Mary Arrigan

maeve ano the goonight trail

The fifth Maeve Morris adventure

Illustrated by Terry Myler

THE CHILDREN'S PRESS

To
Madeline, Frances and Bid

The author wishes to thank
Gay Treacy for the aviation advice

First published 2001 by
The Children's Press
an imprint of Anvil Books
45 Palmerston Road, Dublin 6

1 3 5 6 4 2

© Text Mary Arrigan 2001
© Illustrations Terry Myler

ISBN 1 901737 31 4

Typeset by Computertype Limited
Printed by Colour Books Limited

Contents

1

Charlie

We heard the man called Charlie before we saw him. We heard the scraping of stone on stone, and Leo thought of *The Blair Witch Project (uimhir a dó)* that we'd watched the night before. Served him right really, getting a scare like that. It was he who'd suggested that we explore the grotty old graveyard that we happened upon that afternoon.

Don't get me wrong; it's not that I'm scared of graveyards, you understand, but as far as I'm concerned places like that are best left to the people they're intended for: ie. the dead. Graveyards are OK when you're laying some very ancient personage to rest – lots of long-faced people shaking hands and murmuring stuff that they don't mean, then a quick exit back to someone's house for tea, sambos and foam-filled buns. But this particular graveyard was away out on a rise behind a circle of trees, barely visible from the road and out of shouting distance should there be any weirdness. We had to cross a field to get to it.

'You're not looking out for woo-woo ghosts or anything, are you, Maeve?' Leo scoffed when I hesitated at the crumbling stone wall.

'Don't be such a prat,' I hissed. 'I'm not about to leap over these stupid stones and ruin my good jeans. Cost me a packet, these did.'

Leo grinned and charged ahead, which suited me fine. 'Decorum' was my new mantra. That means being cool and, above all, I wanted to be dead cool – as befits a poet of my stature. A natural literary queen really, as I found myself thinking more and more like a poet. My brain was constantly ticking over with poetic stuff, like finding words to rhyme with other words. That's why most pictures you see of poets show them with a frown – it goes with all the thinking.

We were staying with Leo's distant aunt that Easter. His step-father's sister.

'My step-aunt,' Leo said.

'No such thing,' I said. 'Whoever heard of a step-aunt?' But I didn't push it because I was glad to be asked. Poets are always open to new experiences – it's to do with being madly creative. Anyway, it turned out that we were being sent mainly to keep this step-aunt company and give her a hand in the craft shop she was setting up. Why us? Well first of all, young relatives, however distant, work for peanuts. And secondly, it was seen as an opportunity for Leo to bond with his step-dad's family. The step-aunt's name was Ragnell. Daft name, I thought, until I learned that it comes from Arthurian times. The original Ragnell was married to Sir Gawain, one of King Arthur's knights. Of course that made me look at her in a new light – Pre-Raphaelite paintings of dreamy maidens and macho knights and all that.

But I digress, that has nothing at all to do with the events that followed. Except, maybe, for the *knight* bit, in a roundabout sort of way. We helped in the craft shop in the mornings, Leo and I. In the afternoons we were left pretty much to our own resources. The upside was that Ragnell delighted in taking us around like real adult tourists when she was off work. That included late movies and posh nosh. As a holiday, this one was bouncing along nicely, thank you very much.

When I caught up with Leo he was standing still, listening. He put his finger to his lips as I reached him. 'Give it a rest, Leo,' I said in my best superior voice. 'I'm way beyond your childishly pathetic attempts at scaremongering.' I was just wondering to myself, in poetic mode, what sort of a word would rhyme with 'scaremongering' when he put his hand on my arm.

'Hear that?' he whispered, his face white and set to 'very scared' mode. His fingers tightened on my arm. I was drawing myself up to say something really scathing as I unwrapped his fingers, when I heard it. A scraping sound. I swallowed back the words and sent messages to my feet to be ready for take-off. Scraping sounds are not scary, but here in this isolated place they were creepy.

The noise stopped and Leo looked at me. I knew what he was going to say.

'Be dead quiet,' he whispered. 'And let's have a look.'

The scraping started up again, coming from beyond a ruined chapel that was covered in ivy and half submerged in whispery grass. Before I could stop him, Leo was making his way between the drunkenly leaning tombstones (note the poetic bit there). With a sigh, I followed him. If anything was to happen to the little creep I'd get the blame because I have a couple of years on him. Why couldn't we just run away and have a giggle when we'd reach the comfort of the road? But that's Leo, he'll charge into any dodgy situation, scary or not. We eased our way around the chapel, stepping carefully over bits of shattered glass from the windows.

The scraping was louder now. I swallowed again, this time to banish the image of some skeletal hand scratching to get out. Not very grown-up, I know, but at times like that the imagination can go into overdrive. Leo stopped at the corner and put his finger to his lips again. Together we peered around. Just behind a yew tree we could make out a figure stooped over one of the tombstones, scraping and stopping to brush away the debris.

'It's just some bloke,' Leo said, sounding like he wasn't sure whether to be relieved or disappointed.

'Well, what did you expect – old Drac himself?' I hissed. We didn't feel the need to hide any more so we swished our way through the long grass towards the tomb-scraper. He looked up, startled, when he heard us. Our eyes locked, as they say in the best romances. This creature was anything but dead and skeletal. Every poetic thought I'd ever had in my whole life rushed into my head. His straight, black hair was tied back in a ponytail which made him look real bohemian and romantically offbeat. If this was Victorian times I'd have swooned in a floppy faint.

THE TOMB SCRAPER

By Maeve Morris

Alone, he scraped the mossy grave,
Alone and looking very brave.
His eyes met mine, and then I knew
That here beneath the crooked yew,
Love had blossomed like a rose
That snorted backwards up my nose.

'Pardon the intrusion,' I said, proud of my quick thinking use of properly impressive words. The moment was spoiled, of course, by Leo's loud interruption.

'What're you doing?' he asked, up front and ignorant.

The man smiled and stood up, stretched himself to ease his back. His face was roundish with a very square

jaw. 'Hi,' he said, ignoring Leo and looking straight at me. If love was a lightbulb on top of your head, mine would be flashing like a lighthouse gone mad. 'Name is Charlie. And I'm not a grave vandal,' he added, laughing. 'Despite what it seems.'

Grave vandal? He could demolish the whole topsy-turvy bunch of mouldy old tombstones and dance on the rubble as far as I was concerned. His American accent raised images of pools, sunshine and those cool shopping malls that are all glass and class.

'What are you doing?' Leo asked again.

Charlie threw down the flat stone he'd been using and wiped his hands on his jeans.

'Wasting my time by the looks of things,' he said, nodding at the stone he'd been stripping.

'Why?' went on Leo, peering closer at the tombstone.

Charlie shook his head. 'I've been looking for a name,' he said. 'Carstairs. James Aloysius Carstairs.'

His ancestor, I supposed. I could never quite see the sense in people coming back from better places and plusher lifestyles to mooch about for their long-dead ancestors. Ancestors generally left saintly Erin's dreary shore because they were dirt-poor and always wet and hungry. Who'd want to trail back over that depressing background, for goodness sake? Not me, that's for sure. I sometimes wished my own ancestors had had the guts to up sticks and head for exotic places, or better still, be transported to somewhere like Australia for bopping some po-faced Lord Uppity-Drawers on the head.

THE ANCESTRAL EMIGRANT

By Maeve Morris

Great Grandpa was so poor it hurt.
He grovelled daily in the dirt
Searching for a healthy spud.
'Blast!' he cried. 'No bloomin' good!
I'll pack me bags and leave this life,
Get meself a wealthy wife.'
And so he sailed to USA
Got lots of sun and mucho pay.
'Life,' he said, while sipping beer,
'Is infinitely better here.'

Leo knelt down beside the tombstone and leaned so close his nose almost touched the illegible writing.

'Can't make it out,' he admitted. 'What made you pick this one over all the others?'

Charlie shrugged his pair of shoulders that looked like the products of daily workouts. I made a mental note to make use of Mam's keep-fit books. Not for shoulders, of course. Whoever heard of a poet with *shoulders*?

Charlie smiled. American teeth, of course, *ping!* white like a row of fridges in a fridge factory.

'Well, I'm just chancing my arm,' he said. 'I don't even know if it's the right graveyard, but I have a hunch it is. It's certainly the oldest one around. The dates seem to stop at the early nineteen hundreds. The newer grave-yard on on the far side of town starts later. No good to me.'

'We could help,' I said, my mouth finally in working order. 'Leo and me, we could help you to find your ancestor's tomb.'

Charlie looked at me, and again I thanked God for not giving us lightbulbs on our heads. 'That's very kind of you,' he said. 'Are you sure? I'd really appreciate it.'

I pushed my chin up in what I hoped was a gesture of nonchalance. 'We've nothing better to do,' I said. 'Have we, Leo?'

At first I thought Leo was going to slam my offer with an idiotic suggestion of some other groan-making activity like the hill-walking or pony-trekking he'd been going on about. But he nodded.

'That'd be cool,' he said.

We took a tombstone each and set to with flat stones to scrape the moss from them. My blue nail varnish got seriously chipped, but I knew that Charlie would simply read this as a symbol of my devotion.

'Very English names, these,' Leo called out as he scraped at his fourth tombstone. 'And they've all got bible words at the bottom.'

'What do you mean "bible words",' I asked, glad for an opportunity to pause.

'"Safe in the arms of Jesus,"' replied Leo. 'And "Abide

with me" and "Underneath are the everlasting arms."
Those sort of bible words.'

Charlie laughed. 'You're right about the names,' he
said. 'Most of those people would have been landowners
in the seventeen and eighteen hundreds.'

'Irish Catholics weren't allowed to own land,' I put in.
Sometimes it pays to listen in history class, even if you're
only drawing cartoons of teachers at the same time. 'So,
are we looking for the tomb of a wealthy Protestant
landowner?'

Charlie shook his head. 'Not quite sure about the
religion,' he said. 'Sometimes emigrants came back and
bought land.'

'And is that what he did, this ancestor of yours?' I
asked.

'My ...?' he said vaguely. Then he stopped abruptly,
stretched his arms and looked at his watch. 'I've had
enough. Thanks for your help, you two.'

'How come you know so much about our history?' I
asked, just to prolong the time spent with this hunk. 'You
being American and all.'

Charlie smiled. 'It's what I do,' he said. 'I'm a histor-
ian, a sort of people-researcher. Look, can I give you a
lift anywhere – while I still have the hired car? I've to take
it back to Athlone today.'

'That'd be grand,' I said quickly, in case Leo opted for
another canter through jeans-destroying terrain.

2

Ragnell and Dave

Ragnell was out picking up litter from in front of her shop when the car pulled in. She looked up with surprise as Leo and I got out, and came over to investigate.

'Hello,' she said, peering in to see who was dropping us off.

'It's OK, we haven't been abducted by a weirdo,' I laughed, seeing the 'I'm-responsible-for-these-kids' look on her face. 'This is Charlie. We found him in a graveyard.'

I could see she still wasn't happy. 'He's American,' I went on.

'Looking for ancestors,' added Leo.

'Aren't they all,' muttered Ragnell. 'Were you never told not to get into cars with strangers?'

'Sorry. My fault,' said Charlie, leaning across so that she could see him. 'They generously gave me a hand to scrape a few tombstones,' he went on. Then he held out his hand. 'No harm done, eh?'

The fridge-factory teeth did the trick. Ragnell smiled as she reached in to shake the proffered hand.

'No harm done. Thanks for leaving them home.'

Charlie leaned further and looked up at the shop. 'Nice place,' he said. 'Is it yours?'

Ragnell nodded. 'Craft shop. One week open and patiently waiting for the rush.'

'She doesn't have to wait,' put in Leo. 'Loads of people came to buy stuff already. It's the best craft shop for hundreds of miles.'

Ragnell laughed indulgently, but I could see that she was pleased with what Leo said, even if it was bending the truth a bit. Well, more than a bit, actually. It was a big lie. Customers so far were as scarce as hens' teeth.

'Maybe I'll visit then,' said Charlie, putting the car in gear. 'I like craftsmanship myself.'

'The official opening is tomorrow night,' I hinted, willing Ragnell to invite Charlie along.

'You could come,' said Leo eagerly. 'Couldn't Charlie come too, Ragnell? There'll be loads of people and wine and cheese things.'

Thank you, Leo, I thought. It's good to have an up-front kid with you at times like this.

Ragnell shrugged. 'One more won't make much difference. You're welcome to come along, Charlie.'

'Thanks. I probably will.' And he was gone. I had an empty feeling as I watched the car drive away.

'Bet he just said that,' I muttered.

'Said what?' asked Leo.

'About coming to the opening. I bet that was just *plámás* and he won't come near the place.' It was only when I had it said that I realised I was handing Leo ammunition for goading me. Why did my mouth always charge ahead of my mind? Would I ever master the art of synchronising both?

'Ooh! Maeve's in luuuve!' he laughed, hand on the spot where his heart would be – if he had one.

'Give over,' I growled. 'He's interesting, that's all.'

Ragnell cut in before Leo could come up with another stupid remark. 'Dave has asked us all out for a meal tonight,' she said. 'What do you think?'

'Deadly,' said Leo. 'Burgers or posh?'

'Posh,' laughed Ragnell. 'Means washing behind your ears and wearing a tuxedo.'

'Huh?' said Leo, aghast.

'Just kidding. About the tux, that is. You'll still have to wash behind your ears though.'

'Are you sure he doesn't mind us tagging along?' I asked, with sensible and mature understanding of things romantic. 'Surely he wants a cosy evening with just you and him?'

Ragnell snorted. 'You're my guests. Where I go, you go.'

Poor Dave, I thought. Ever since we'd come to stay with Ragnell he always seemed to be at the end of her phone or popping in to buy something crafty which, any eejit could see, he was only buying as an excuse to be in her presence. He was about thirty-five and lived with an aunt in some big old house outside the town. He was what my mother would call an eligible bachelor, but what I'd call a stay-at-home mammy's boy. If I were thirty-five and as rich as he was I'd be off doing Caribbean cruises and stuff like that. I really admired the way Ragnell kept him at a distance, which only served to have him dance attendance all the more. I made a note for future reference. Dead cool, that's how I'd be when some Romeo's hormones focused on me. Dead cool, poetic and oozing decorum.

DEAD COOL LOVE

by Maeve Morris.

My love keeps knocking at my door.
'Away,' I cry. 'Come back no more.'
That really drives him mad with zeal.
'Oh please,' he says.' Know how I feel.
I love you, with your manner cool.
I love the way you make me drool.

> *I love your poems and gorgeous face.*
> *Your great decorum, slinky grace.'*
> *But I can make him toe the line.*
> *So I grudgingly agree to dine.*
> *That's the way to keep men hopping*
> *And pay the bills when you go shopping.*

Frankly I'd have preferred a burger joint myself. There's a lot to be said for being able to sink your molars into a bun and meat and lick tomato sauce off your fingers without the hassle of sniffy waiters and fear of dribbling some highly-coloured sauce on the tablecloth. But against that there's a lot to be said for prawn cocktails and tall desserts dripping with choc sauce. So I mended the chipped nail varnish and wore my sequinned top.

'I never saw rainbow-coloured chainmail before,' laughed Leo. 'You going jousting, Maeve?'

I just gritted my teeth. That's where the decorum bit comes in. However, when he made a stab at me with a pretend lance, I let him have it – a beautiful stinging blow on his left ear that stopped the insults in mid-stream. That was when Ragnell wafted in, smelling of *Eau d'Issey,* and found the snivelling child clutching his ear.

'Maeve!' she said. 'Really!'

I started to defend myself, but it wasn't worth the effort, especially as she'd gone to stand beside the window to watch for Dave.

'Isn't that him?' said Leo, running over to the window and pointing to the headlights of a car that was pulling up outside.

'Yes,' replied Ragnell, pulling him away. 'Don't let him see you.'

'Why?'

'Because we don't want him to think we've been waiting for him.'

'Why? That's what we're doing.'

'Because … that's how it is. Wait until he rings the bell.'

It rang. Ragnell didn't move. She looked over at me and winked. In that intimate, sisterhood moment I felt I was a truly grown-up woman. I winked back, acknowledging the power we girls wielded, at the same time wondering what we'd do if Dave simply went away. The bell rang again and Ragnell moved to the door. I scrutinised Dave's face to see if he minded Leo and me tagging along, but he seemed OK with the arrangement. Just as well; I was starving.

3

Romance and Posh Nosh

The restaurant was one of those small plush places where they take your coat and you don't see it until the end of the evening. Leo said that was to stop people doing a runner, but I told him not to be so common. Which was rather spoiled by Dave saying that Leo was quite right.

'They put microchips into the lining of the coats when they hang them up,' he whispered. 'Especially anoraks, because you can't trust anyone in an anorak. Then, if you try sneaking out without paying, the microchip sets off a screaming alarm. That's when the heavies make a beeline for you and you end up being blacklisted from every eatery in Ireland.'

'Wow, wicked!' said Leo.

'He's sending you up, Leo,' laughed Ragnell.

'Good idea though,' said Leo. 'I'll tell Jim to get some of those microchips.'

'No fear of anyone doing a runner from his place,' I said. 'The sort of veggie geeks who go there are too nerdy to try anything that daring. Too puny from eating carrot tops and hard beans.'

Oops! That was my mouth acting without my permission again. There was an ominous silence at the table. Jim is Leo's step-dad, Ragnell's brother. He's married to my aunt Brid and they run a vegetarian restaurant in a one-horse midlands town called Kildioma.

Die? I wanted to disappear in a puff of sequins. I was conscious of Leo's snarl. That I could cope with. I hadn't the nerve to see how Ragnell was taking my back-firing put-down that was an insult to her brother. When I heard a tinkling sound, I looked up in amazement. She was laughing! Was it at me or with me? It didn't matter so long as she wasn't throwing sharp cutlery at me with dire warnings never to darken her shop again.

'That's our Jim,' she said. 'Grew up saving injured animals. Always bringing home some half-squashed hedgehog or broken-down bird to nurse back to health. Fitting, isn't it, that he's making a living *not* using dead animals.'

Nice one, Ragnell, I thought. With a few simple words she'd smoothed over any threatening prickles. After that I minded my Ps and Qs and the evening romped along. Dave was funny with Leo and me, but he was really only using our laughter to impress Ragnell. However, there was no question about it, he impressed Leo and me out of our heads when he mentioned his plane.

'Your what?' asked Leo, gawping like a fish.

Dave smiled. 'Just a small Cessna 172,' he said.

'Wow!' drooled Leo.

Well, I must admit to drooling a bit myself, but at least I didn't have chocolate sauce dripping down my chin.

'You'll come for a trip one day soon?' went on Dave.

Leo swallowed loudly. 'Sure will,' he gasped.

I would have shrieked and jumped about, but for the decorum thing. Instead I knocked over my glass which was an accident and doesn't count as lack of decorum at all.

'You see?' Dave said, leaning towards Ragnell. 'See how your young relatives are charmed by my wealth and personality. How come you're not bowled over by all I have to offer? Come with me and we'll travel around the world. I'll write travel books and you can mix my cocktails, cook my ... no, no, I mean you can sun yourself and bathe in warm pools.'

Ragnell laughed and waved dismissively. 'Cool it, you big braggart,' she said.

Dave looked at Leo and me. 'I've been trying to get this woman to marry me,' he said. 'Wouldn't you like a nice day out? See your aunt in a fairytale frock swanning down the aisle to her Prince Charming – that's me ...?'

'Stop right there,' said Ragnell, beginning to look slightly embarrassed. 'I have no intention of swanning down any aisle in a white meringue, and as for a prince, charming or otherwise, no thanks.'

'Aw, come on, Ragnell,' went on Dave, with exaggerated pleading in his voice. 'Gimme a break. What does a bloke have to do to prove undying love and devotion?'

By this time Ragnell was really embarrassed. I couldn't believe this was happening right in front of me – a real proposal. It was like one of those momentuous events that you read about but think you'll never witness, such as the birth of a baby – or an alien in your shed. Leo was pretty gobsmacked too. We didn't know whether we should say anything or not. I mean I was all for telling Ragnell not to be an eejit and take the man and his plane. I would, if it was me.

'This isn't the time,' she said, glancing sidelong at me and Leo.

'Oh, but it's the very best time,' said Dave, moving back his chair. 'Right here, in front of witnesses. Will you marry me, Ragnell, and make an honest man of me?'

'If you make a show of me by going down on one knee, I'll empty that jug of water over your head,' whispered Ragnell. She turned to us, still with our mouths open. 'Don't mind this messer,' she said. 'He goes on like this all the time. Get up, Dave. People are looking.'

'That's why I'm doing it,' said Dave, with a flamboyant wave of his hand. 'How can you refuse a public declaration of love, especially in front of family members?'

'Get up, you fool.'

'Say it, then.'

'Say what?'

'Say yes.'

Ragnell frowned, then laughed. 'All right. Yes. There I've said it. Now get up.'

'Wow!' Leo gasped. 'Does this mean that you're engaged?'

'I suppose so,' muttered Ragnell.

'Oh, it does, it does,' said Dave. 'Can't back down now, lady, or I'll have you up for breach of promise.'

'Is that it, then?' I couldn't help asking. 'Is ... is that all there is to getting engaged?'

Ragnell laughed and touched my arm. 'Look, we've disillusioned Maeve,' she said. 'No soft lights, music and flowers. Not very romantic, is that what you're thinking?'

I didn't know how to answer that, but I would have thought there'd be a bit more to a proposal than a threat of cold water.

'Don't worry, Maeve,' she continued. 'Dave has tried all that. He's realised the only way to get me to marry him was to embarrass me into it. And it worked.' Then, by the way she looked at him, I knew everything was all right. 'Just one thing,' she said, getting serious again.

'Oh, oh,' groaned Dave. 'There's a catch? What is it? No more beer? Change my socks more than once a month? You've got it, babe.'

'Shut up and listen to me,' said Ragnell. 'I don't want you to tell Cass. Not yet.' She turned to Leo and me. 'Dave's aunt is a bit on the sharp side. Don't think she

quite approves of me.'

'She's a raving virago.' added Dave. 'And it doesn't matter what she thinks. She doesn't approve of me either.'

'Well, not a word, OK? We'll get round to telling her soon.'

Dave nodded. Then he brightened. 'This calls for a celebration. Who'd like an Irish coffee?'

'With whiskey in it?' I asked.

'It's the only way I know how it's made,' said Dave.

'Wow!' Leo and I looked at one another with amazement. This was real living.

'Just a tiny drop of whiskey for these two,' Ragnell whispered to the waiter when Dave ordered the four Irish coffees. Just her gesture towards doing the auntie thing, I thought.

They do that, aunts. It goes with the territory.

Was this grown up and oozing sophistication or what! I glowed as I played with the creamy white head of cream that topped the glass, putting off the moment when I'd have my first sip just so that I could anticipate it a bit more. And I knew from Leo's beaming face that he was bursting with glee. Except he didn't have the gift of genteel anticipation like me.

'Don't gulp, you guzzler!' laughed Dave. 'You're supposed to sip slowly.'

'That's Leo,' I put in, my quick wit flashing as usual. 'A true lager-lout in the making.' Well, you have to make the most of these opportunities when they present themselves.

Later on, back at the house, we were in my room, Ragnell and me – women together for woman-talk. Leo was downstairs fiddling about on the computer. I wanted to get the low-down on what it felt like to be suddenly engaged and all that. But before we could get stuck in, we were interrupted by thundering footsteps on the stairs. Leo burst in, face beaming.

'There's an e-mail from Jamie!' he exclaimed. 'He's in Ireland!'

Suddenly my heart's a-leaping! Jamie is a very good friend. He lives in England, but his grandfather lives in a big house near where Leo lives. Jamie spends a lot of holidays there, so we get to meet a few times a year. When we first met Jamie we thought he was a toffee-nosed wimp, but now he's turned out to be a dishy fourteen-year-old with trendy hair and clothes with cool labels. I take the credit for that, of course. Snigger at a bloke's fair-isle jumper and ancient hairstyle and he'll either go under or take your well-intentioned jeering to heart. Luckily he'd done the latter. Take a bow, Maeve.

'Is he with his grandfather?' I asked, sitting up.

'Here, I printed it up,' said Leo, handing me the sheet. I read eagerly.

'Yo, Leo,' it said. 'Back in the old sod for Easter. Your ma says you and Maeve are away *working*! Major disappointment. Looks like I'm doomed to a boring time here. Probably give grandpa the privilege of a few days of my company and head back to queen and country. Love to Maeve. Jamie.'

'Oh no,' I groaned. 'Jamie's in Ireland and we won't get to see him. Blast!' I wanted to pack up right there and then and hitch a lift back to Leo's place. Could I bribe Leo into pointing our way towards home? Feign a sudden life-threatening and highly contagious ailment?

'Who's this?'Ragnell asked, peering over my shoulder at the e-mail.

'Jamie,' Leo said. I was too choked up for words. 'He's our friend, me and Maeve's. We hang out together when he's in his grandpa's, back in Kildioma.'

Ragnell looked at me. Eyes, shoulders, elbows, knees – everything – must have been drooping with the disappointment of missing Jamie.

'Must be special, judging from the faces of you two.'

'He is,' sighed Leo. 'He's our best friend, Jamie is.'

I nodded in agreement.

'So you'd like to go home and spend the rest of the holidays with him?'

My face did a quick upturn, and I was about to say yes, yes, yes! when Leo shrugged. 'No, it doesn't matter,' he said as he took back the printout. 'We'll probably see him in the summer.'

Summer! That was several lifetimes away. My mouth opened and shut as I silently swore at Leo. Trust him to ruin the moment.

'Is he house-trained, this Jamie?' asked Ragnell.

'Huh?' Leo and I said together.

'Does he break furniture? Slobber cans of coke all over the carpet? Have anti-social habits? Could he be trusted with a knife and fork?'

We gaped at the woman. Trust Leo to have a mad relation, however distant. Maybe getting engaged had turned her brain to slush – they say big moments can do that. She laughed at our puzzled faces. 'Well? Isn't anyone going to answer?'

I giggled at the image of Jamie smashing chairs and slobbering.

'Don't be daft,' said Leo scornfully.

'Just kidding,' said Ragnell. 'Why don't you ask him here for a few days?'

'Wow! Do you mean that?' I asked.

Had I heard properly or were my ears making up words they'd like to hear?

'Sure. There's plenty of room. Is he useful?'

'Oh he is,' I said, bursting with goodwill towards this cool lady. 'Jamie could organise your whole shop, no problem, and sell stuff to people who didn't know they wanted it. You could trust him with ... your whole life.'

'Well, I don't think we'll need to go that far, Maeve. Set it up there, Leo. E-mail back and ask him to come. Turn off the lights before you go to bed. I'm off to get my beauty sleep. Good night.'

'She's one amazing lady, your Ragnell,' I said to Leo when she'd gone.

'Of course she is,' he snorted. 'She's related to me, isn't she?'

Eh, no actually, I was tempted to say, but this time the mind got there ahead of the mouth to shut it up. No point in antagonising the lad when everything was going my way.

'Do you think he'll reply straight away after you send the invite?' I asked.

Leo shrugged and looked at his watch. 'Half-eleven. Depends on whether he checks his e-mails. Probably not at this hour.'

'Oh, no!' I moaned. 'That means we won't know until tomorrow.'

'Maybe not even then,' said Leo. 'He mightn't log in for a couple of days. Not everyone checks their e-mails every day, you know.'

I prepared to moan again, but caught his gleeful expression as he enjoyed my anxiety. How could I sleep tonight wondering if Jamie was coming or not?

'If he doesn't come you'll have to be content to chase Charlie,' said Leo.

But I knew that he was just as eager as I was to have Jamie here with us. I plonked back on my pillow and wished.

4

The Grand Opening

It wasn't until midday next day that we got Jamie's e-mail. Needless to say I was like a jittery flea all morning, constantly running into the office to check for e-mails. When it did come, of course it was Leo who got it. When he called out to me I abandoned the green vase with a drippy design that I was wrapping for someone, and ran back to read the message.

'Great. Really chuffed to be asked. Grandpa says he'll give me a lift. We should be there about lunch-time tomorrow. Keep any action until I arrive.'

Action? There *was* no action. We were pottering in the shop in the mornings and mooching about the locality in the afternoons; not mind-shattering stuff. Oh lord! I hadn't thought of what we might do. Maybe Jamie would be bored to death and the whole visit would go up in smoke. I made a total hames of wrapping the vase, but I was way beyond caring. Jamie was coming. I smiled at the customer and told her to keep her hand under the bottom of the box.

Ragnell closed the shop for the afternoon, and we spent several exhausting hours getting ready for the opening. Tables were set out for the stuff that the deli was to deliver. We hung dried flowers and ribbons all around the walls, and put loads of aromatic candles everywhere, ready for lighting just before opening time. Later on Dave let himself in to lend a hand.

'Point me in the direction of hard labour,' he said, taking off his jacket. 'Let a man at the work.'

29

'We have nearly everything done,' said Leo.

Dave laughed and ruffled Leo's hair. Not a good idea to ruffle the hair of a skinny little kid who thinks he's a macho man. Leo reached up and ruffled Dave's hair.

'Yecch,' he exclaimed with great exaggeration. 'Sticky gel.'

If Dave was annoyed, he disguised it well. 'Good job I wasn't wearing a toupee,' he said.

We did some more finishing touches to the place. I felt it was a pity that a mob would be coming in soon to mess up our good work. 'The place looks smashing,' I said. 'It's just brilliant.'

'Yes, it is,' agreed Ragnell. 'Let's hope that people will turn up now.' I hadn't thought of that.

'What will we do if nobody comes?' asked Leo. 'With all the wine and cheesey things?'

Ragnell laughed. "We'll have to eat it ourselves. For the rest of your stay we'd have cheese and pâté for breakfast, dinner and tea.'

At five-thirty the deli delivery came and we put out the film-wrapped finger food and glasses for wine. Ragnell, Leo and I went to change out of our jeans. I could have hugged Ragnell when she told me I looked great in my sequinned top. Jamie was coming, the opening was going to be exciting, and I'd look my best. Ragnell even gave me a spray of her *Eau d'Issey*. I felt good.

The first guests began to wander in shortly after six. The wine was poured, cling-film whipped off the nibbly things, and before long the place was humming with life. Everyone brought a good-luck gift, but it was Dave's gift that made us gasp. He fetched it from his car and presented it with a flamboyant gesture.

'I've been dying to give you this all afternoon,' he said. 'But I thought it would be more fitting to present it at the official time.' It was a feathery thing trimmed with beads and metal bands.

'What is it?' I asked.

'It's a fan,' replied Ragnell, her usual cool demeanour replaced by pleasure and amazement at this weird gift.

'Very old,' put in Dave. 'It's been in my family for years. Thought it would be suitably crafty to hang in your shop.'

'It's ... it's beautiful,' murmured Ragnell. 'I'll treasure it always.'

'What's this?' asked a strident voice. 'What's that fan doing here?'

We looked around as a very thin lady elbowed her way towards us. Think of an anaemic prune with a frown and you've got her. This could only be The Aunt. She confronted Dave, ignoring Ragnell, Leo and me, and pointed to the feathery thing. 'What's this doing here?' she said, all wobbly neck and anxious eyes.

'It's all right, Cass,' said Dave placatingly. 'It's just that old fan that's been hanging in the drawing-room for years. Isn't it better off decorating Ragnell's craft shop than just being a dustcatcher at home?'

'Oh no, not the fan,' the old lady said pleadingly. 'You had no right. It's a family heirloom, that fan.'

'Oh, for heaven's sake, Cass,' groaned Dave. 'What can you possibly want with...?'

'Please,' put in Ragnell, 'let's not quarrel over it. Take it back, Cass. I'm sure Dave didn't want to offend you. Here, please take it.'

But Dave put his hand on her arm. 'No, Ragnell,' he said, his eyes defiantly on the aunt. 'It's mine and I'm choosing to give it to you. You must keep it.'

Oops, this could get a bit hairy, I thought. I grabbed Leo's shoulder and propelled him back into the crowd.

'What did you want to do that for?' he said. 'I was enjoying that.'

'Nothing to do with us,' I said virtuously. 'No point in us standing there gaping like two dummies. Take one of those plates and see if you can shovel more grub into this lot. I don't want to end up feeding on leftovers for days, like Ragnell said.'

Leo snorted, but did as he was told. I took another plate and circulated through the crowd. This is a very clever thing to do at parties because that way you don't get stuck with people who'll numb your mind and cause you to drop down with boredom. Unless, of course, they turn out to be people that you really do want to be stuck with, in which case you simply stay put. But there weren't many of those there – people I'd have liked to be stuck with I mean. They were mostly past their sell-by date and their chatter was definitely not mind-blowing. When I glanced over to check how Ragnell was holding out against the ranting aunt, I was pleased to see Dave standing on a stool pinning the fan to one of the beams that crossed the ceiling. Good, I thought. Game, set and match to Dave. However, my pleasure was short-lived when I saw the aunt making a beeline for me.

'You must be Ragnell's niece,' Cass said, fixing me with her glittering eyes. Now I knew how a rabbit must feel when caught in headlights. I froze and waited for the impact, willing a group of hungry people to surround me and feed off the plate of curling nibbles I was holding.

No such luck. 'How lucky she is to have you and your brother to come and help her,' was her greeting.

Well I couldn't have her think Leo was my brother, however much I wanted to get away.

'He's my cousin,' I said. 'And I'm not actually related to Ragnell. My aunt is married to her brother, that's all.

Would you like one of these things, missus?'

She waved away the plate I'd stuck under her nose. Horror of horrors, she put her hand on my shoulder and drew me to her in a conspiritorial manner. 'So, tell me all about your family,' she said. 'Pretty girl like you, tell me about yourself. And please, call me Cass.'

Well, this wasn't too bad. I marvelled at her switch from witch to luvvie. Perhaps I'd misjudged the old dear. Maybe Dave was really at fault for giving away the family feathery thing. So I found myself telling her about me and my poems, my family and Leo's family. She nodded and smiled and encouraged me along avenues of thought and opinions which tripped so easily off my tongue. I was quite comfortable with her as we chatted away and the nibbles got curlier and curlier. I felt I'd scored over Ragnell in the charm stakes. If this aunt was supposed to be prickly, then it was probably because people didn't know the right way to flatter her, as I did. Well, as you would humour someone who says you're pretty.

'Look who's here.' Leo's voice cut into our cosy chat. I looked up to see him leading Charlie towards me. Charlie, all teeth and tan and tee-shirt. My heart did a bit of a flutter. But, as far as my responses went, put an 's' where that first 't' is and you get 'fluster', because that's what happened; I got completely flustered and dropped the nibbles right over the floor. Leo laughed, but Charlie immediately bent to pick them up and Cass helped. I was so out of my head with embarrassment and confusion that I actually offered him one of the nibbles that we'd picked off the floor.

'And are you going to introduce me to this fine gentleman?' said Cass, taking the plate from me and pushing it under a table. My head shifted gear to a normality of sorts.

'This is Charlie,' I stuttered. 'And this is Cass.' They smiled and shook hands.

'Charlie's looking for his ancestors' grave,' said Leo.

'Not quite, Leo,' laughed Charlie. 'Just doing a spot of research, that's all.'

'You're American?' said Cass. Her eyes narrowed a bit as she leaned towards Charlie and peered at him short-sightedly. Was it my imagination or did she pale slightly? 'And your ancestors came from round here?'

'Carstairs,' put in Leo. 'Isn't that the name you were looking for, Charlie? On the grave,' he added as Charlie didn't respond. 'Weren't you looking for...?'

Cass looked surprised, her hand went to her wrinkled throat as she continued to stare at Charlie.

'No, Leo,' said Charlie. He seemed to be uncomfortably aware of Cass's eyes fixed on him. 'You must be mistaken.'

'But I'm sure you said ...'

Charlie shook his head. 'Perhaps that was the name on one of the other tombstones we were looking at,' he murmured. I was about to put in my spoke and agree with Leo, but maybe Charlie was right. Maybe it was simply a name that had come up.

'So what name were you looking for?' asked Cass.

'Knight,' answered Charlie.

Cass shook her head. 'Never heard of any Knights around here,' she said. 'Perhaps you're in the wrong place?'

Charlie just gave a kind of a smile and shook his head.

Cass excused herself and disappeared into the crowd. Charlie looked around at the chattering crowd. Talk to me, I wanted to say. I searched for something really original to say to this pony-tailed hunk, but any good stuff was lying at the bottom of my brain. Maybe something about the weather would get us on to world-shattering conversation about eco things and holes in the sky. 'What's the weather like where you come from?' I began.

Charlie's face froze. Oh lord, I thought, I'm being a bore. Come on brain, you can do better than that. But his eyes were fixed on something behind me. I turned. All I could see over the heads of the guests was the fan as it gently swayed back and forth where Dave had hung it.

'Where did that come from?' he asked in a low voice. 'That fan?' Then he intoned some word that sounded like 'payout,' but since that made no sense, I figured I'd imagined it.

5

Jamie

Dave came around next morning to give us a hand with the clean-up. The rent-a-glass people had been around earlier, so we were just left with the ground-in pastry crumbs and half-eaten nibbles to scrape up. I kept checking my watch. Would Jamie ever arrive?

'What time did he say he'd be here?' I asked Leo.

'I've told you umpteen times, Maeve. Around lunch-time.'

But what was lunch-time? It could be twelve o'clock, one o'clock – anything up to half past two. I looked at my watch once more. Twelve-fifteen. Would my hair and face last for another couple of hours before wilting?

'Is Cass speaking to you again?' Ragnell asked Dave, pointing to the fan.

'Bit of a lip this morning,' laughed Dave. 'But she'll get over it. I must say that fan looks just right hanging here in your craft shop.'

'It does,' agreed Ragnell. 'Still, if ever you want it back...'

'Fat chance,' said Dave.

'She's really a nice lady, your aunt,' I said. 'I got along fine with her.'

'Must be your charm, Maeve,' smiled Ragnell. Well, of course it was, but I'm not one to boast.

Dave was about to say something when Leo let out a cry and ran to the door.

'It's Jamie! Jamie's here!'

The decorum I'd been carefully saving for this

moment was replaced by panic. Did I look all right? What would I say to him? Please, God, don't let me blush. God must have been out to lunch just then because I could feel my face ignite into an inferno of hot red. I put my hands to my cheeks in an effort to cool them. Ragnell saw the gesture. 'You look great,' she said as she followed me to the door. 'Dead sexy.'

Sexy? My da would have choked at the idea of me being described like that. It was a constant struggle between me and my da – him wanting me to stay in girlie gear and pigtails until I'd be forty-five, and me a devout fashion victim. Luckily Mam was a bit more enlightened and went along with my whims. She said that fathers don't like to see their daughters grown-up, that it made them, the fathers, feel old.

But there, I digress again. I was chuffed at Ragnell's remark and felt better about going to meet Jamie.

Jamie and his grandad were getting out of the car, Leo flapping around them like a moth to a light. When all the hand-shaking and introductions had been made, Ragnell invited them both in for coffee. Mr McLaren shook his head as he unloaded Jamie's rucksack from the boot.

'I'm heading for Cork,' he said.

'For horses?' asked Leo.

'For horses,' laughed Mr McLaren.

'Horses,' Jamie laughed, looking at me. Mr McLaren breeds the things. Jamie knew my thoughts on horses – high, nerve-racking and hazardous things that are only waiting to toss you into muck or kick you with those dangerous feet. I laughed back. Now the ice was broken and we could get on with the holiday. Jamie seemed to have got more grown-up since I last saw him. Perhaps it was the number one haircut that did it. Very macho. Leo pushed past me and threw himself at Jamie.

'You came,' he said gleefully. 'Now the holiday will be perfect.' My sentiments exactly, but I didn't say so. Decorum, you see. It had found its way back.

After we'd waved a cheerio to Jamie's grandfather, we all went to the kitchen for lunch.

'Leftovers, I'm afraid,' said Ragnell. 'Good pâté, some smoked salmon, mushroom vol-au-vents, and whatever else survived the night.'

It didn't matter. I'd have eaten stale crusts and parsnip mush I was so pleased. That is until I saw the approving look on Jamie's face as he spoke to Ragnell. She's too old for him, I told myself. Anyway there was Dave to cancel out any attraction there. Think cool. But I had acted before the thought reached my brain. 'Dave is Ragnell's fiancé,' I said, patting Dave's arm.

'Huh?' said Dave.

'Maeve!' said Ragnell.

'You big nellie,' laughed Leo. 'It's a secret.'

'Oh, forgot. Sorry. But Jamie won't tell, will you Jamie?'

Jamie shrugged. 'Who would I be telling?'

Dave laughed and the moment passed. But at least I had put things in proper perspective as far as Jamie was concerned. Like, I was to be the only woman on his horizon.

That afternoon, Jamie wanted to browse around the shop, so we told Ragnell that we'd look after it while she took an hour or so off. It was while we were in charge that Charlie came in. More blushing and fluster on my part. Especially when I saw Leo nudge Jamie and make soppy eyes while nodding towards me. Let them. I'd show them.

'Charlie!' I beamed, charming as you like. 'Nice to see you again.'

'Are you going to the graveyard again, Charlie?' asked Leo.

Charlie shook his head. 'No. Finished with that part of my investigations.'

'Charlie is looking up his ancestors,' Leo explained to Jamie. 'Isn't that right, Charlie?'

Charlie smiled and looked hastily around the shop. 'I'd like to buy some crafts to take home,' he said.

'Well, you're in the right place and I'm the right person to help,' I said.

He settled for coasters with a celtic motif. Cheapskate stuff, though it seemed to me he was buying just for the sake of buying something. Just like Dave. Then it hit me; was he smitten by Ragnell too? That came as no surprise. And the added romantic aspect almost caused me to swoon when it occurred to me that, with a name like

Knight, he was just right for Ragnell. It was like an Arthurian love story set in 2001. And I couldn't even tell him she was hitched

THE DARK KNIGHT

By Maeve Morris

The knight who came to find his roots
Instead found love. With merrie hoots
He wooed the fair and lovely maid
Whose hair hung long in yellow braid.
'I love you, Rag,' he said. 'Forsooth,
I'll fight for you with nail and tooth.'
'There is another!' the damsel cried.
And, curling up, the knight he died.

Even as I was wrapping the coasters, Charlie was looking about, almost nervously.

'She'll be back shortly,' I said helpfully.

'Who?' he looked at me with surprise.

'Ragnell,' I went on giving him what I hoped was a knowing, understanding grin.

'Really?' his pretended lack of interest only showed up his ardour all the more, I thought. Then he pointed to the fan that was hanging from the beam. 'How much for that?' He nodded towards it.

'Oh, I couldn't sell that,' I said. 'That was a gift. It's only for decoration.'

Charlie sighed. 'Well, I'd pay a very good price for it,' he went on. 'I'd pay fifty euros.'

Fifty euros! For a feathery fan that had been gathering dust for years? Hang on, Maeve, was it *me* he was trying to impress by offering mega-bucks? Wow! I wanted to call the boys over. What to do? Wouldn't Ragnell be pleased if I produced a fifty-euro sale!

'Well?' he said. 'How about it?'

'You'll have to ask Ragnell herself,' I laughed. 'I couldn't sell it without her permission. It was a gift from a friend.'

'I'd really like to have it,' he said. 'I'll pay you what ever you ask.'

'I couldn't, Charlie. Honest. Isn't there anything else you'd prefer?'

'No.' Charlie's chin stuck out with determination. 'That's really what I want, that fan.'

I shrugged and made a helpless sort of gesture.

'Too bad,' he said, turning to leave.

'Your coasters,' I called out.

'What?'

'You were forgetting your coasters.'

'Oh. Yeah. Thanks.' He took the package, not even noticing the little ribbon I'd stuck on, and was gone.

'Strange,' I said to Jamie and Leo later. 'He seemed almost annoyed that I wouldn't sell the fan.'

'Americans,' snorted Jamie. 'The "I want" race.'

Still, I was puzzled. For the short time I'd known Charlie, this act didn't sit comfortably.

6

Goodnight House

Later on Leo and I took Jamie to see the town.

'It's not as if there's much to see,' I said apologetically. 'Up one side and down the other and that's it.'

'I like little towns,' said Jamie. 'In Britain there are hardly any left. They've all got too big and impersonal. Small towns like this have character.'

'Character?' I laughed. 'I've seen more character in a shoe box.'

'Yeah, well we don't all come from Gotham City like you,' muttered Leo. 'Snobby old bat.'

The three of us turned when a car horn honked behind us. 'It's Cass,' said Leo. Sure enough Cass was peering at us over the steering-wheel of a dust-covered Opel Astra.

'Admiring our town?' she called out, lowering the window as she drew up beside us. I was about to say something sharpish and scathingly funny about the town, but decorum got there ahead of the mouth again. The downside of decorum, though, is that you have to keep your great lines to yourself, which isn't half as much fun.

'We're showing our friend Jamie the sights,' I said.

'Come and see Goodnight House, where I live.' said Cass. 'That's really the only decent place in town.'

Well, the choice was either humour the old woman and see some place new, or mooch about the streets in search of rivetting action. As if.

'Sure,' I answered for all of us, and we piled in on top

of the shopping. 'Great name for a house.' Well, weird
really, but the woman had said I was pretty, so why
shouldn't I humour her?

'It is,' agreed Cass. 'And who is this young man?' she
asked, turning dangerously away from the road to peer at
Jamie.

'Jamie,' said Leo. 'He's English. He's our friend, me
and Maeve's.'

'Hello,' Jamie nodded.

It was a relief to all of us when Cass switched her
attention back to her driving. 'And what about your
other friend?' she asked.

'What other friend?'

'The American chap. Looking for his ancestors.
Where is he?'

'He's around,' Leo shrugged. 'He's probably gone
back to the graveyard.'

'Oh?' Cass wiped the windscreen that had got fogged
up since we'd got in. In the mirror I could see her frown
(not a poetic frown of course – that's an entirely different
sort of frown), putting extra lines on the prunish
forehead. Maybe she felt the same as I did about people
digging up ancestors.

By now we'd reached two piers with carved horses'
heads on top. 'Goodnight House' was written in a
wrought-iron arch above them, just like those mega
ranches in western films. There was a big sweep of
avenue ahead, a long clump of trees on the right.

'The river flows on the other side of the trees,' said
Cass. 'We used to swim there as children. You can too,
if you like.'

'Bit early yet,' I replied, giving an involuntary shiver.
'It's only Easter holidays, not summer.'

'Soft,' muttered Cass. 'Modern kids are soft.'

We wisely let that pass, knowing that to defend our generation would only bring a catalogue of 'when-I-was-your-age' examples.

The house was indeed impressive. It had those pointy gothic windows with latticed glass and a parapet on top with castellated stonework. There was a turret with a round roof, a balcony over the wide front door, and gargoyle things on either side of the windows which could have been portraits of ancestors for all I knew. Maybe that explained the prune complexion. A hard house to draw, if you were into that sort of thing, there were so many curly bits and in-and-out angles.

'Cool,' I said.

'Strange mix of architecture,' said Jamie. Well, he should know. His ma draws houses for a living, being an architect. Cass looked at him sharply. 'I mean it's a very interesting looking house,' he added diplomatically.

'Built by my great-great-grandfather Carstairs,' said Cass proudly. I could see the woman was totally immersed in the bricks and mortar of the place.

'Is your name Carstairs too, you and Dave?' exclaimed Leo. Cass nodded. We hadn't known Dave's surname. But then, you never use people's surnames except on formal occasions and, with Dave, nothing was ever formal. No wonder she'd reacted like she did when we mistakenly thought that Charlie had been looking for the same name. Nobody would want strangers appearing on the doorstep suddenly claiming the same dead ancestors. Confused coincidence.

Cass led us into the front hall and waited for us to admire. What to say?

'It's like something from *Gone with the Wind*,' I said.

'That's it,' put in Jamie. 'Almost American colonial.'

We smiled at one another, pleased that we were saying

the right things. That usually earns a bit of eating and drinking. Sure enough Cass led us to the kitchen and poured us some lemonade from the fridge.

'I make it myself,' she said. 'Good for the skin first thing in the morning.'

It certainly tasted like something that would cause your skin to pucker into a prune, and I made a note to avoid anything to do with lemons in the morning or at any other time of day or night. However it gave me great pleasure to see Jamie and Leo trying not to screw up their faces in reaction to the tarty drink.

Afterwards Cass brought us on a tour of the house. It was big, boring and draughty. The drawing-room was huge. I couldn't envisage anyone curling up here to watch *Home and Away* unless they had one of those stripey beach shelters to go around the sofa.

'This is where that fan used to hang,' Cass said,

pointing to a spot over the piano. 'For years and years it hung there – from long before I was born.'

'You grew up here?' I asked.

'Of course I did. Dave's dad was my brother.'

'And have you lived here ever since?' I went on.

Cass shook her head. She paused, as if trying to put the words together. 'I left when I was young. I only came back several years ago.'

'From where? Did you get married?'

Well, they're the sort of questions a poet should ask. It's important to be interested in people's lives because that's how you get the ideas for poems. How else could that wedding guest in the Ancient Mariner have got the makings of that long poem about a ghostly ship if he hadn't stopped to talk to the old beardy guy?

Cass smiled. 'You ask a lot of questions, dear,' she said. Then she pointed to the fan spot again. 'I really miss that fan. I don't think Dave should have given it away. Don't get me wrong,' she added hastily. 'I love your aunt's shop. It's very pretty. But don't you think the fan is out of place there? It's much more suited to an old room like this.'

Leo and I shifted a bit uneasily. Jamie, of course wasn't aware of the bitter exchange between Cass and Dave last night. I was getting bored with the whole fan thing and tried to change the subject. 'Bet this place is cold in winter.' The words were out before I realised. Wrong words.

'Don't be ridiculous, child,' Cass scoffed. 'This room is quite cosy. That fireplace throws out very generous heat.' Yeah, if you threw in a tree and a coal mine or two. But I didn't say that.

As if on cue, the door opened and an oldish guy struggled in with a bucket of briquettes and an armful of wood. He looked at us with surprise.

Cass smiled. 'This is Simon, our right-hand man. These young people have come to admire the house, Simon.'

Simon gave us a brief look. I recognised him from last night at the opening. I remembered thinking him a spooky type, just taking in all the action but not talking to anyone.

'Hello. Welcome to Goodnight House,' he drawled.

Another Yank! Was there a box of Yanks somewhere in the neighbourhood, I wondered, being let out in ones and twos to infiltrate and conquer the boggy midlands? Eye contact and merry chat were not high on this guy's list. We went back to the kitchen where Cass offered us more of her homemade acid. Needless to say we declined. 'We'd better be off,' I said, looking at my watch but not really noticing the time because it was only a ploy to leave. Cass nodded, but didn't offer to drive us the mile or so back to town. She came to the door with us. Then she leaned towards Leo.

'That fan,' she began. I groaned to myself. Not that again. Leo gave her a suspicious look. 'Perhaps if you explained to your aunt about it being an heirloom and how you've seen the spot where it's been hanging all these years, she might come round to letting an old lady have it back, eh?'

Leo looked at me for guidance. I shrugged. Let him sort it out; after all Ragnell was his half-aunt or whatever. 'I'll ... I'll ask her,' he muttered dubiously.

'Good man,' said Cass. 'Use your gentlemanly powers of persuasion.'

I covered my mouth to stop any loose remarks from getting out in response to that nugget of fancy. Even Jamie was smirking. Before we turned to go down the long avenue, I happened to glance at the big drawing-room window. Simon was there, gawking out at us. When he saw me looking, he ducked back into the room.

'Weird,' I whispered to the others.

'Which thing did you have in mind in particular?' laughed Jamie. 'There was a lot of weirdness about.'

'That Simon,' I said. 'He was just standing there, staring at us.'

'Probably doesn't get to see much company out here,' said Jamie.

'All he needs is a bolt through his head and heavy boots,' put in Leo. 'Maybe the old lady invented him in a cellar – an Irish Frankenstein.'

'Bet she feeds him with that toe-curling juice she makes,' I said. 'That's probably what's wrong with him. Poor beggar, we shouldn't be laughing,' I added, just to put me on a higher moral level and make me look kind and good. 'Maybe he's just shy...' I broke off and stopped. We were in sight of the gates with the big wrought-iron arch.

'Isn't that Charlie?' I said.

The boys followed my gaze. 'Where?' asked Jamie. 'I can't see anyone.'

'He was there, looking up at the sign,' I went on. 'I saw him. I'm sure it was Charlie.'

Leo snorted. 'Your imagination has got the better of you, Maeve. Just because you saw one old geezer at a window, you'll be seeing blokes everywhere. Get real. Look, there's nobody there.'

We'd only gone about a hundred yards down the road when Charlie stepped out from behind some trees. The three of us jumped.

'Charlie!' I exclaimed. 'How did you get here ahead of us? I saw you just moments ago at the gates. You frightened the lives out of us, you spooky thing.'

Charlie laughed and tapped the side of his nose. 'Old tracking trick,' he said. 'Ancient skill.'

'Neat,' said Leo. 'Can you show me, Charlie?'

'Sure thing,' replied Charlie. 'Come into the trees and I'll show you.'

So, for the next hour or so, we made our way back to town the rough way, with Charlie showing us how to track down one another without cracking a twig or rustling the undergrowth. We got the hang of it after a while. Well the boys did. I wasn't that much interested in mincing around behind trees anyway. Big waste of time, but it kept the macho men happy. Me, I'd have preferred to be sitting somewhere upbeat with Charlie, finding out about him and about life in the States, practising a bit of Ragnell-style cool, and maybe wangling an invitation over.

'This is deadly, Charlie,' enthused Leo. 'Where did you learn all this?'

By now we'd reached the town and, thankfully, a man-made road. Charlie tapped the side of his nose again and laughed before heading towards the hotel. 'See you folks,' he said.

'No you won't,' Jamie called back. 'Not the way we'll creep up on you, Charlie.'

Charlie laughed again and waved. 'Don't forget the secret of tracking,' he said as his parting shot. 'Think like a shadow.'

7

Shock at the Shop

We went to the cinema that night. Dave and Ragnell dropped us off at the multiplex before joining some of their own friends in the hotel bar. Needless to say I'd have preferred if it was just Jamie and me going to the movies, just like a regular date. I had thought of bribing Leo to stay home, but I knew that wouldn't work for two reasons: (a) Ragnell wouldn't have agreed to that, and (b) Leo, being such a pain, would have me paying for the rest of the holiday. So it was a case of making sure the little prat wouldn't sit between us. As it happened Jamie plonked himself in the middle. That was a relief.

We had tried to get into an over-fifteens film, just for the fun of it. But the snooty bird perched at the box-office took one look at Leo and shook her head. So we were stuck with a U certificate mush. I didn't care, though. I was sitting with Jamie, elbow to elbow. Thank God elbows don't blush. The night was promising. Come on, Christina Ricci up there on the big screen, I thought, set the scene for a bit of romance.

I nearly lost my reason when I felt Jamie nudging me at the first bout of on-screen snogging. This was it! He was finally declaring his love for me. I nudged back. Yes, no mistake, there it was again, a definite nudge. I sighed.

Then it happened again, at the next snogging incident – a definite nudge. I nudged back, just to show that I too was feeling the romance of the moment. But next time, I thought of Ragnell and how she'd treat this declaration of love. Cool. Detached.

LOVE DECLARED

By Maeve Morris

They sat together in the dark
She trembled like a captured lark.
'I love you, Sweet,' the youth did sing.
'Please take this fancy diamond ring.'
'I love you too,' the maid replied.
'I'll love you till we'll both have died.'
Their lips did meet, like wobbly jelly.
Her ice cream melted on her belly.

I leaned towards Jamie and whispered; 'I understand how you feel, Jamie. But we mustn't rush this.'

'Huh?' he looked at me in the gloom. Then there was another nudge. Jamie sniggered. 'Give over, Leo. Maeve has something to tell me. Go on, Maeve.'

I swallowed very hard. If I could have swallowed my whole face I would have done. The nudges were coming from Leo! All those times I'd thought Jamie was nudging me at the romantic bits, it was Leo acting the maggot by shoving Jamie who in turn was pushed against me.

'Maeve?' prompted Jamie.

'I … Nothing,' I replied. Please, God, don't let him have heard. Let him have been smitten by temporary deafness just like you smote all those people in the bible and they weren't even nudging.

'You understand what?' he whispered.

'Shut up and watch the film,' I hissed, face pointed at the screen as though I was really interested, but seeing nothing because my eyes were screwed up with embarrassment.

I could feel Jamie's eyes peering at me. I could sense his grin. The prat, he'd heard all right. The rest of the film just passed me right by. I was dreading the moment when the lights would go up.

Cool. Think cool.

As it happened it was Leo who saved my face by tumbling head first into the next row down by trying to leap over the seats. Jamie and I pulled him up and untangled his legs, which made us all giggle and forget the nudging incident. 'Amnesia, God,' I mouthed to myself. 'You opted out of the deafness request I politely made, so at least have the good nature to impose a bit of amnesia.' You'll notice the frequent chatlines to God – that's because I'd discovered that poets always talk to the highest authority. We'd arranged to meet Ragnell and Dave in a coffee shop near the cinema. Every table was occupied. Even my icy stares didn't succeed in shifting any of the layabouts who were chatting loudly.

'They won't be along for ages yet,' said Leo. 'It's only half ten. What'll we do?'

'We could go to the hotel bar,' I replied. 'I'm not going to hang around the dreary street while this lot take up tables. Let's go to the hotel and cadge some coke and crisps from the half-aunt and her fancy man.'

'Or an Irish coffee,' suggested Leo, smirking.

But Jamie had a better idea. 'We could have coffee in the hotel lobby,' he said. 'That way we'll be warm and on the spot, and just have to wait for them instead of muscling in on their date. OK?'

We were lucky to get a small table near the fire in the lobby of the beautifully named Grand Hotel. Grand? Think brass, dark wood and dark Victorian velvet. Dark and heavy. Think a setting for a horror movie.

'I'll bet this place hasn't had a facelift since the days of coaches and blokes in wigs,' I said.

'It's nice,' said Jamie. 'Old-fashioned.'

'There you go again,' I muttered.

'Excuse me?'

'It's all you ever do. Any time I point out something that's seriously lacking, you come up with "It's nice." If there weren't people like me to note these things, nothing would ever change.'

'If there weren't people like you, there'd be a great lack of moaners,' put in Leo. 'Moan, moan, moan. Moaning Minnie, that's you.'

OK, so I was tired, cold, and still smarting from making an eejit of myself over the nudging incident, but I suppose I needn't have stomped on Leo's toe. It was a low, mean and uncool act. Very satisfying, though.

His yell brought over a skinny guy in a brocade waistcoat and a badge with 'Liam' written on it.

'What's going on here?' he growled.

'It's this poor lad,' I said, batting the eyelashes. 'He's

hit his shin on the corner of that fiddly little table. You really ought to get better quality furniture. But we won't sue. You don't want to sue, do you, Leo?' I asked sweetly. Leo scowled. Jamie spluttered.

I turned my attention back to the string-bean with the badge and acne. 'Pot of coffee for three and a few bickies, Liam. Thank you very much.' No move from the lackey. 'We're waiting for Dave Carstairs,' I said, an inspired flash. 'Mr Carstairs with the plane and the big house. He's eng ... going out with this chap's step-aunt Ragnell. You know? The new craft shop? They're meeting us here shortly.'

With a shrug, he shuffled off to meet our needs.

'Staff,' I snorted. 'No class these days.'

'Like, if it was you you'd be flouncing about dancing attendance on customers?' scoffed Leo. 'I don't think so, Maeve. You'd put the run on them before they'd have parked themselves.'

There was a groan from Jamie.

'Don't you two ever grow up?' he said, with a tad of bad humour. 'For as long as I've known you, you're forever sniping at one another. Boring.'

That stopped Leo and me in our tracks. My first reaction was, naturally, to say something defensive and offensive and put Jamie in his place. But I realised that his place was where reason and maturity reigned, so I swallowed back the words. We sat down, silenced and nobody said anything. Me, because I was afraid I'd say the wrong thing; Leo because he was too gobsmacked by Jamie's rebuke; and Jamie because he was still annoyed.

Leo fidgetted, shifting on the leather sofa and making squeaky noises. He stopped suddenly.

'Look,' he cried. 'There's Charlie.'

Sure enough, Charlie was crossing the lobby in the

reception area. He stopped briefly, said something to the receptionist and headed for the revolving door.

'Charlie!' I called out. But he had already disappeared.

'Wonder where he's going at this hour of the night,' said Leo. 'He was carrying a bag.'

'Late-night shopping at the twenty-four hour mall?' I said.

'Don't be daft,' laughed Leo. 'There's only a small Super-Valu supermarket here. Shuts at five.'

'I know,' I said. 'Joke, Leo.' I made a mental note to upgrade my jokes in case people thought I was really an airhead – there being a very fine line between genius and idiocy. Still, I wondered where Charlie was heading off to in such a hurry at ten past eleven. 'A quick drink in a pub before closing time?' I wondered aloud.

'Us?' said Leo, eyes wide.

'No, you wally. Charlie. Do you think he's heading out for a drink before closing time?'

'Why would he do that when there's a bar here?' said Jamie. 'He could even have it through room service if he wanted to.'

'Maybe he doesn't like the atmosphere here,' I suggested. 'Bit drab, huh?'

'So, why bring a bag?' asked Leo.

'Smuggle back some fish and chips?' said Jamie. 'Beef curry to have in bed?'

Just then Liam, he of the brocade waistcoat and stringy body, shuffled back with the coffee and bickies. He hung around until we paid him, which made us giggle as we counted out the money in small coins. The coffee tasted like it had been stewing since early morning – and probably was. But did I say this aloud? Like hell I did! I didn't want to cause another battle of words. Decorum, you see.

THE MARTYRED BEAUTY

By Maeve Morris

She suffered all the awful food,
The grotty caff, the waiter rude.
She smiled real sweetly at her beau.
'How nice,' she said, her cheeks aglow.
And though the grub was deadly foul
Did she rant or did she growl?
Like hell she did, the perfect lassie
She kept dead cool and very classy.

It was nearly twelve before Ragnell and Dave sauntered out of the bar. They were surprised to see us. Dave ordered more coffee and Ragnell said he must have something going with the kitchen staff to be able to get coffee at that hour. A torn fringe on one of the curtains was flapping about a bit. Dave frowned.

'Getting up a bit of a wind,' he said. 'I'd better ring Simon and see if he'll push the plane into the hangar for me. Won't be long.' He rushed off.

So we chatted to Ragnell and told her about the movie – three different versions of course.

'It was interesting,' said Jamie.

'Brill,' enthused Leo.

'It was crap,' I said.

'Too many chases for Maeve,' laughed Leo.

'Too right,' I muttered. 'Brilliant dialogue – if you like gallops and grunts.'

'What's keeping Dave?' said Ragnell, looking at her watch. 'He's been gone ages. He's only making a call from his mobile. Why didn't he ring from here.'

'Some people like to make their calls in private,' I said. 'I know I do. I can't think properly if there are people around while I'm making a call on my mobile. I usually go into the loo or stand in a doorway.'

With that, Dave came back. 'Sorry about that,' he said.

'Did you get him?' asked Ragnell.

'Get who?'

'Simon.'

'No, he wasn't there. I'll have to do it myself when I get back. How about a bite to eat? I'm starving.'

However, as it turned out, food was the last thing on our minds when we reached Ragnell's place.

'There's something not quite right,' she said, looking around the small front hall that led to the kitchen at the back. We followed her down the passageway. Sure enough there was a cool draught coming from a gaping hole in the glass panel of the back door. Ragnell paled.

'We've been broken into,' she said as she turned and ran to the door that connected the house to the craft shop. We all gasped when we reached it. Things were strewn around the floor. But, strangely, nothing seemed to be broken. Ragnell ran to the till and opened it.

'Was there money in the till?' asked Dave. 'How many times have I told you to clear it at the end of each day…'

'It's all right,' Ragnell put in. 'I had just left about twenty euros worth of change.'

'Is it gone?' I asked.

She nodded. 'Hardly worth their while to break in,' she said. 'Better check the rest of the house.'

But nothing had been disturbed. We marvelled that whoever broke in had left the telly, video and music centre. Nothing in any of the upstairs rooms had been touched either. Still, I was glad that I'd hidden my poetry copy-book under my mattress. No point in leaving stuff lying around that would be priceless in a few years' time – though it was mainly to hide it from Leo.

We made our way back to the shop. Ragnell surveyed her stock as we replaced things on shelves. She shook her head. 'I don't understand,' she said. 'Nothing seems to be missing. It's very strange. Spooky almost. Why break in and not take anything?'

It was when I looked above her head that I found that at least one thing had been nicked.

'Your fan,' I cried. 'Dave's fan. Look, it's gone!'

The gardai came pretty promptly after Dave rang them. Needless to say they got their knickers in a bit of a knot because we'd put our fingerprints everywhere.

'Are you sure there was nothing of value taken?' one of them asked.

Ragnell shook her head. 'Just the small amount of cash in the till, and the fan.'

'Was the fan of great value?' the garda continued.

Ragnell looked at Dave. He took up the answering. 'It was just an old fan that I gave Ragnell to decorate her shop. Been in my family for ages, but it couldn't be of any value. It was just a bunch of feathers and leather.'

The garda frowned. 'Could it be a practical joke?'

Ragnell shrugged. 'Some joke! Who'd want to break in for a joke?'

'Break out, you mean,' said another garda who had been mooching around the kitchen.

'What do you mean?' asked Dave.

'Whoever did this didn't get in through the kitchen door. That glass was broken from the inside to make it look like a break-in. It was either someone with a key, or else someone who's very expert at stealth.'

At that, Jamie, Leo and I exchanged worried glances – were each of us thinking the same thing?

8

Trouble!

Later on, after the gardai had gone, Jamie, Leo and I went to the kitchen to make tea while Ragnell and Dave finished cleaning up the shop.

'What do you think?' I asked as I filled the kettle.

Jamie shrugged, said nothing as he put out some mugs from the dresser.

Leo snorted. 'Charlie wouldn't do that,' he said.

'But he was pretty insistent that he wanted that fan,' put in Jamie. 'What was it he offered, Maeve?'

'Fifty euros. He must have been pretty desperate to offer that much for a moth-eaten bunch of feathers.'

'But he'd never break in,' said Leo. 'Not Charlie.'

'Who else would want it?' asked Jamie.

'Cass,' said Leo. 'Didn't she almost strangle me to death to get Ragnell to give it back?'

Jamie and I laughed. 'Yeah, Leo,' I chortled. 'Like, the old lady doubles as a cat burglar! Get real.'

Leo looked suitably sheepish. 'Could've hired someone to do it.'

This time Jamie and I howled. 'You reckon she's some kind of rural Godmother?' said Jamie, adding in a Bronx accent. '"Hey, Alfonso, you gotta break into de craft broad's shop and get me dat fan, ya hear?"'

We smothered our laughs when Ragnell and Dave came in. Dave went over to the broken panel on the back door. 'Garda's right,' he said. 'All the shards of broken glass are outside. But how did whoever it was get in? Is there anyone else with a key?'

Ragnell shook her head. 'Just you,' she said. 'I gave Dave a spare key to the shop because he was helping with the moving in,' she added, looking at us. I knew she was explaining that in case we'd think it was for snogging. Which is exactly what I thought anyway, until I realised that the door between the shop and the house needed another key. Big disappointment; I'd have liked to think of Dave tip-toeing in for a bit of romance. But that's the poet in me, you see.

'And you have that key safe?' asked Jamie.

Dave smiled and put his hand in his pocket. Then he tried the other pocket, then the inside pockets. His smile changed to a look of anxiety. 'Dammit! I always carry it around with me. I know I had it in this jacket.'

'When did you last have it?' asked Ragnell.

Dave frowned. 'Yesterday, before the launch. I let myself in, remember? While you were setting up. The shop was locked and I let myself in. That's the last time I had it. I distinctly remember putting it back in my pocket. Same jacket.'

'You had your jacket off,' I put in. 'You were in your shirt all evening.'

Dave slapped his hand to his forehead. 'You're right, Maeve,' he groaned. 'I left it on a chair somewhere. Anyone could have lifted it. With a big crowd like that, anyone with a bit of stealth could have lifted it. Blast.'

Stealth! That very descriptive word again. Jamie, Leo and I exchanged glances once more. Charlie! Could he actually have been setting out, that time we saw him in the hotel, to rob Ragnell? He would have seen her and Dave at the bar.

'Should we tell the gardai?' Leo asked later that night when the three of us got together in my room to talk things over.

Jamie shook his head. 'Let's hold on that for a while,' he said. 'Tomorrow we'll innocently call to the hotel and make like we want to hang out with him.'

'Won't that make him suspicious?' I asked.

'Not really,' replied Jamie. 'We got on so well at the tracking that we can pretend that we want to find out more.'

'That's true,' Leo said. 'It would make sense. And it would make us seem real friendly. Lull him into being pally and he might let something slip.'

'Or we could tie him to a tree and make him confess,' I put in. 'Torture never goes astray. Bit of eye-gouging or fingernail-pulling and we'll have him confessing to anything we like. I fancy a bit of torturing. I think I'd have made a dead cool torturer for the SS or the Spanish Inquisition – you know, those guys with long frocks and thundery faces who wanted everyone to bow to their religious power. Although, personally, I would never have been one to give in if it was me being tortured. I'd have stayed calm and silent no matter what they did to me.'

The two boys looked at me, jaws slack and eyes wide.

'Close your daft gobs,' I said. 'You look stupid, the pair of you. Do I have to explain my superior humour? Huh?' They were still staring. 'What's your problem?'

Leo began to snigger, Jamie began to smile. I realised they weren't looking directly at me, their eyes were focused somewhere over my head.

I whipped around to see what they were staring at. A huge spider was suspended above my head, abseiling his hairy-legged way towards me. My arachnophobia kicked in. I don't want to dwell too much on my reaction because there was no decorum at all in my screaming and tearing about. Perfectly natural response, of course.

But it didn't help that Jamie and Leo had to hug one another – not out of fear, but to hold one another up as they laughed helplessly. Jamie wiped the tears from his eyes and caught the spider in a tissue.

'Don't kill it,' I said, from a safe distance.

'I could torture it,' he said. 'Force it to give state secrets away.'

I would have scowled at the poor attempt at a joke, but my eyebrows were still stuck way up my forehead with fear. Leo opened the window and Jamie deposited the creature on the sill.

'Make sure that window is closed tight,' I muttered, which caused them both to snigger again.

'Oh, grow up,' I said, trying to restore my dignity.

'Sorry,' said Jamie. He patted my hand. 'Are you OK?'

Any other time I would have swooned with delight, but I had just been through a terrible trauma which kind of put the gesture on the back burner. 'Let's get back to what we were talking about,' I said gruffly. 'Charlie.'

I knew Leo was dying to make some remark about my boast of not giving in to torture, but Jamie shut him up.

'I was saying,' said Jamie, 'that we'd call to the hotel tomorrow and meet up with Charlie. Right?'

Leo and I nodded. 'I still don't think it was Charlie,' I said, yawning. 'Robbers don't show you how to track and they don't have fridge-factory teeth.'

'Probably not,' agreed Jamie, looking puzzled, but I hadn't the energy to explain my logic. Anyway I wasn't quite sure where that bit of logic came from. 'But we'll make sure.'

That night I dreamed of fridges, spiders, Charlie and the word 'payout'. That's dreams for you – a whole heap of garbage running riot inside your head.

9

Where's Charlie?

The Grand Hotel looked even gloomier in daylight. The fire in the lobby hadn't been lit yet, which gave it a sort of extra dreariness. Liam, the string-bean, was polishing tables with an energy that would have done justice to a tired tortoise. The receptionist, all suit and starch, looked up from her computer and tried to look as though we were interrupting an international booking of World Leaders into The Grand.

'Excuse me,' said Jamie. We'd made him spokesman because of his posh accent. 'We want to see Mr Knight.'

'He's gone,' she replied.

'Gone? Gone where?' I asked.

'I wouldn't know,' said the receptionist. 'Even if I did, it's not our policy to give out information about our guests.'

'When did he leave?' asked Jamie. 'This is very important.'

The receptionist sighed and looked at some book on her desk. 'Last night, apparently. Eleven-ten, that's what's down here.'

'But he must have left some forwarding address.'

The starch creaked as the receptionist leaned towards us. 'Look,' she said, 'I'm only filling in here while someone is out sick. I don't know where your friend Mr...' she looked again at the book, '... Knight is. And I don't much care. I'm just doing a job for the day, so don't ask me to keep track of people, because I have no idea. Right?'

Her attitude got right up my nose. 'Well, you should keep track,' I said coldly. 'This boy,' I put my hand protectively on Leo's shoulder and pretended to gulp back emotion. 'This boy is his son who has come to stay with him for a few days. Why would Mr Knight arrange to have his child come here and then shove off before the kid arrives?'

That certainly caught her attention. But the moment was ruined by Leo pushing away my arm and snorting, 'Give over, Maeve.' And the moment was extra ruined by Jamie sniggering into his sleeve.

'I nearly had her,' I growled when we got outside. 'If you two had co-operated she'd have sung. Now we don't know what to think.'

'What is there to think about?' asked Jamie. 'Charlie tries to buy the fan, he's refused, says he really wants it, fan is nicked, exit Charlie. Need I go on?'

I sighed. It looked bleak all right. I couldn't think of one argument against Jamie's words.

'You should have taken the fifty euros,' said Leo.

'Oh shush,' I said impatiently. 'What do we do now?'

'Not a lot we can do,' answered Jamie. 'No way of tracing him. Probably legging it back to the States by now.'

'Wonder what was so special about that fan,' I mused. 'It's not as if it was made of gold or anything. It was just a bundle of moth-eaten feathers and bits of tin.'

'Who knows?' shrugged Jamie.

'Should we tell the others?' asked Leo.

'Ragnell and Dave?' I said. 'What's the point? They wouldn't be able to trace him either. Let's leave it, eh?'

'Ooh, Maeve wants to protect her boy-friend,' tittered Leo. 'Didn't know he was a scanger, did you, Maeve? Trust you to fall for a bloke who nicks stuff.'

I drew myself up to say something defensive and put Mister Little-Bigmouth in his place, but then it occurred to me that I could let Jamie stew with the thought that my affections might lie elsewhere. So I just smiled what I hoped was an enigmatic and mysterious smile.

LOVELY LISA AND THE HANDSOME THIEF

By Maeve Morris

> *'I didn't know,' the maiden cried,*
> *'That my love to me had lied.*
> *I thought I was his lovely Lisa,*
> *That all his gifts were paid by Visa.'*
> *'Not so,' the guard said with a wink,*
> *And clapped her lover in the clink.*

Dave was in the kitchen when we got back. He was fixing the glass panel on the back door. Leo watched him for a few moments. I could see from the thoughtful frown that his mind was ticking.

'Have you no job?' he asked eventually.

Oh, cringe. 'Leo,' I hissed, 'don't you know better than to ask that! Lots of people have no work, it's a sign of the times. That's a very ignorant thing to ask. Sorry about that, Dave.'

Dave stopped what he was doing. 'Not a problem,' he laughed. 'Leo means have I nothing better to do than hang around here? Fact is I'm a lazy sod. I have most of my land leased to local farmers, so that keeps bread on the table and a roof on the house, leaving me time to doss and fix things for good-looking birds.'

'Don't mind him,' said Ragnell, coming into the kitchen. 'Dave Carstairs is no idle playboy. He has a degree in English and writes articles for several newspapers. He wasn't fantasising when he said he wanted to travel and write. He'd be a hands-on travel writer – not like those ones who stay a week in a plush hotel and write about what they see through the windows of air-conditioned buses.'

That bit of passionate defence stopped us all in our tracks. Ragnell got a bit embarrassed when she saw us looking at her. 'Just setting the record straight,' she muttered as she rummaged in the fridge for lunch stuff. Good idea that, I noted. Rummaging in a fridge is a great way of disguising a blush while cooling down at the same time. 'I wouldn't have these youngsters think I'd have a dosser in my life,' she continued, her decorum well and truly back on course. Dave said nothing, but I could see he was dead pleased.

'What are you folks all doing this evening?' he asked.

We looked at one another, Jamie, Leo and me. 'Nothing planned,' I said – carefully in case there was a catch, like work.

'How about you come to my place?'

'Goodnight House,' said Leo.

'That's right,' said Dave with surprise. 'How did you know that?'

'We've been there already,' I put in. 'Your aunt Cass showed us around.'

'She did? I didn't know that.'

'We met Simon,' I added, just for mischief. 'He didn't say much, though.'

'Simon never says much,' said Dave.

'Is he a relation?' I went on, now that the wheels were in motion for extra info. The poet thing again – ask questions and get ammo for great verses.

Dave shook his head. 'Nope. He came with Cass when she came back from the States four years ago. She said he'd worked for her and she owed it to him to bring him along.'

'She lived in America?' said Leo.

'She did. Been around, our Cass.'

'So why would she come back to a pokey little town like this?' I said. 'She could have gone to Florida. Lots of old people hang out in the sunshine in Florida.' Luckily I didn't mention the big, cold house she'd come back to. There's only so much you can say without becoming an enemy of the people.

'Cass would really thank you for lumping her in with "old people",' laughed Dave. 'She fancies herself a sprightly young thing in her sixties. As for why she came back, well I suppose there comes a time when a person wants to get back to roots. Especially when there's plenty of room. Too much cruddy room,' he added. 'Could accommodate every returned emigrant for miles around in that barn of a place and not meet them for a week. Anyway, her business had gone under so she was pretty broke.'

'Though you'd better not say that when you're talking to her,' put in Ragnell. 'Nobody likes it to be known that their business hasn't worked out. I could be in the same position myself if the craft shop doesn't take on.'

We all made polite noises about that never happening and that she was sure to make a go of it and all that sort of palaver. Lies, all of it. Any eejit could see that selling handmade key-rings and lumpy pots in a small inland town wasn't going to make her fortune.

Ragnell smiled. 'We'll see,' she said.

'And if it did fail you could go and live in Goodnight House,' I joked. 'It could become a centre for people whose businesses go under.'

That went down like the proverbial lead balloon. Jamie rolled his eyes to heaven, Leo shook his head, and nobody laughed. Personally I thought it was a very fitting thing to say, but some people just can't keep up with subtle humour.

'You were talking about this evening,' prompted Jamie.

'It's not a dinner, is it?' asked Leo. 'Have we to dress up and all that?'

'Nah,' laughed Dave. 'I thought we'd get in some Chinese and have a game of Monopoly or something. Good old-fashioned board game. No Playstation, I'm afraid.'

Well, that sounded just fine.

10

The Goodnight Trail

There was no sign of Cass when we arrived at the house. I thought she might be doing something old-ladyish like Bingo, but Dave said she was out for her run.

'Run?' I said. The image of old Cass in leggings and headband didn't sit comfortably in my mind.

'Yes,' said Dave. 'She'd be like a bag of cats if she didn't get her five-mile trot every day.'

'You're kidding,' I went on.

Dave shrugged. 'It's true. Now, whose is the King Prawn Chow Mein?'

There was a contented slurping and chomping as we settled into the Chinese grub in the informal comfort of the kitchen.

'Now this is what I'd be doing every evening if I had money,' said Leo.

'Me too,' I agreed.

'And Irish coffee afterwards,' drooled Leo.

We went into the sitting-room to play Monopoly.

'Simon has the fire lit,' said Dave.

Simon looked up when we came in. He nodded and slithered from the room.

'Does he have a coffin in the cellar?' I quipped.

'Simon?' said Dave. 'He likes to potter around in his room. Reads a lot, watches telly, does a bit of net-working. He's quiet, goes his own way and is quite happy.'

Well, that put me nicely in my place. We started to play Monopoly on a big coffee table before the fire. I had the boot, which I thought would bring me luck because it's a thing that they tie to the back of a bride and groom's car to bring them luck. Well, it certainly didn't do it for me. I lost my houses and my one miserable hotel quite early on. Which would make me a candidate for the Failed Business Folks of Goodnight House. I got up and wandered around the vast sitting-room. It was full of the sort of knick-knacks that you'd get in any old house. On a side table there was a whole lot of ancient photographs in silver frames – you know the kind, all brown and faded. Mostly they were photos of lacy ladies with stern faces and geezers with moustaches that must have really interfered with their consumption of soup or ice-cream cones.

'Meet the ancestors,' said Dave. 'I'll join you, I've just lost everything.' He pointed out a photo of a bald old gent sitting on a straight-backed chair. The name JA Carstairs was visible in faded copperplate writing across the bottom. 'He's the man who started all this,' went on Dave. 'My great-great and possibly greater-grandfather. Made his money on the Goodnight Trail.'

'The what?'

'The Goodnight Trail,' went on Dave, as if I should have heard of it. 'Way back in the 1860s cattle drives across the US were big business. Men were hired to herd cattle over long trails. Charles Goodnight was one of the cattle kings who hired them. My ancestor, JA, joined up with Goodnight and made his money as a cowboy.'

'Wow!' I was deeply impressed. 'Imagine having a real cowboy as an ancestor. Cool.'

Dave laughed. 'Not quite the romantic image you get in those old Western films,' he said. 'The work was hard and only the fittest survived. Old JA was more than just a survivor, though.'

'Yeah? How was that?'

'Well, when they'd reach the cattle stations after the long rides, it was customary for the cattle drivers to spend their money on gambling, drink and women.'

'Don't tell me,' I smiled. 'Your old gramps said his prayers, drank his cocoa and saved his money.'

'Right on,' agreed Dave. 'None of your revelry for old JA. Saved every penny. When he figured he had enough saved he came here, to the land his Irish parents had always lamented leaving – they emigrated during the Famine – and built this place. Called it after the Goodnight Trail.'

'He certainly made a statement about his wealth,' I said. 'This house is humongous.'

Dave nodded. 'A lot of money went into it,' he said, 'but not much taste. As a feat of architecture it's tacky. He obviously copied some big house in America. You've only to look at the pillars and porches and big open-plan hall to realise it was meant for a much warmer climate than here. It's a nightmare of a place to spend winter in. Severe-looking character, isn't he? Certainly looks like a man who'd have no time for wine, women and high-stake poker games.'

'Just as well,' I replied. 'Or you wouldn't be here in your big American-style mansion.'

'Could have ended up as a smallholder scraping the soil for a living,' laughed Dave.

'Instead of being a bigholder scraping rent from your *tenants* who scrape the soil,' I put in, which I thought was rather clever. Shame the way real wit often goes unnoticed.

I picked up an old photo that was partially hidden behind the others. It was a faded image of a group of tough-looking men in cowboy gear.

'Goodness!' I exclaimed. 'I've never seen a photo of real cowboys before.'

Dave took it from me and wiped the dust off with his fingers. 'Very old. These guys were mostly a mix of European emigrants, Mexicans, and Native American Indians.'

'Indians?'

'Yes. Colour or race wasn't of any interest to the cattle kings like Goodnight. The old idea of the white man and the Indian being always deadly enemies isn't quite true. So long as a man was tough, an able horseman, and able to herd steers he was hired. ... Now, I'd better get back to make sure those two crooks aren't cheating my beloved. Amuse yourself there.'

I put back the photo and took up another one which showed a larger group. I peered at it more closely. Real cowboys. I wanted to savour their faces, perhaps get inspiration for a poem. A Western Epic maybe. I frowned as I wondered what would rhyme with 'tumble-weed' and 'wagon train'. One figure in particular stood out, even though it was a bit blurred with age. It was a man with a tallish hat with a feather stuck in it. His hair hung in pigtails on either side of his square jaw. So this was what a real Indian looked like. My eyes kept returning to this figure who, for some reason, caught my imagination, made me feel like I'd seen him before. An involuntary shiver crept up the back of my neck.

Just then, Cass came into the room. Sure enough she had on a track suit and running shoes, so Dave hadn't been winding us up. Her eyes swept around the room, taking in all the company and she greeted us all with breathy cheerfulness. 'I see you're meeting the ancestors, dear,' she said to me. 'Must take a shower,' she went on. 'Sweat sure builds up after a five-mile walk.'

'Well, if that doesn't make us all feel like lazy lard-asses,' said Dave after Cass had left.

'Speak for yourself,' laughed Ragnell. 'I need all my energy to buy property on this board. I think you boys will have to concede that I've won.'

'Afraid so,' said Jamie.

'Because we let you,' added Leo. He ducked as Ragnell went to hit him with a wad of Monopoly money.

I was relieved the stupid game was over. I hate games where you're kicked out for not being good with figures. And I'm not – good with figures that is. Words that rhyme, that's where my genius lies. I'll bet Christina Rossetti or Elizabeth Barrett Browning weren't much good at sums either. It's all to do with different parts of the brain. I'm dead lucky that the poetic part of mine is so phenomenally creative. You don't achieve glamorous fame by knowing how to do hard sums. I went back to studying the photo in my hand, trying to imagine what life was like for those men way back then on the cattle trail.

Simon came in to say that there was tea in the kitchen if we'd like some.

'Great, Simon. Well done,' smiled Dave. 'Come on, folks. There's probably cake as well. We keep a good larder here in Goodnight House.'

Simon nodded and set about stirring the fire into life. No doubt he was dying to get us out of the room so that he could tidy up after us.

Cass joined us for tea. She made no mention of the fan, and nobody squealed that it had been nicked. I was only sinking my teeth into the second slice of lemon cake when Leo dropped the clanger.

'Where will you live, Dave?' he asked, his eyes focused on the cream he was scooping from the cake.

'What?' Dave looked startled.

'When you get married, where will you live? Here or in Ragnell's?'

Think about a deathly silence. Now add a volcano grumbling to erupt. That was the scene. I kicked Leo under the table. At first he scowled at me, but then he realised what he'd said.

Maeve to the rescue. Well, I tried. 'Don't mind him,' I said, my voice coming out as a high-pitched screech. 'He's mixing you up with someone else we know who's getting married, isn't that right, Leo? Isn't that right, Leo?' I said even louder because he was just cowering there like a vampire who'd discovered he was caught out in daylight. But the damage had been done.

'What's the boy on about?' asked Cass.

Dave gave Ragnell a helpless look before facing his

aunt. 'I meant to tell you this evening,' he said. 'I've asked Ragnell to marry me and, well, she's finally said yes...'

He broke off when Simon dropped the milk jug he'd been holding; his face had paled to an even whiter white. Jamie and I leapt into action to clear the mess – well, not so much that as to get us out of the line of fire. We tried to make like we weren't part of the group, like you'd be when your best pal is getting a telling-off from her ma and you try to look invisible. Leo, on the other hand, just sat and watched, head turning from one to the other like people at a tennis match. I tried to catch Leo's eye to scowl at him that this was all his fault, but he didn't look in my direction, not once. Simon had his head in his hands. Well, I suppose you would when you'd just dropped a full milk jug at a crucial announcement. From under the table we sensed Cass's silence, Jamie and me. Yes, that's what I said – *sensed*. You could almost touch the heavy silence.

'I see,' she said eventually. 'Well, I suppose congratulations are in order. When is the big day?'

'Oh, we haven't decided on that yet,' said Ragnell. 'It's hardly even official yet, the engagement.'

'Well, just give me plenty of notice,' the old lady went on, her voice hollow. 'I'll need to find a place to live.'

'What?' said Ragnell. 'What do you mean?'

Jamie and I felt it was time to come up for air. I was amazed when I saw Cass's face. It was like watching a thunder cloud gathering. Wow, I was glad it wasn't me on the receiving end of that response.

'You'll hardly want me here when you move in, dear,' went on Cass.

'I ... no ... I mean of course you'll stay on,' stuttered Ragnell. 'Heavens, there's no question of...'

'We haven't even got the ring yet,' put in Dave. 'Stop jumping way ahead, Cass. You won't be put out on the side of the road. Don't worry.'

Cass's mouth drooped. I prepared myself to hug those bony shoulders and be the kindly young thing with the heart of gold. Or rather, be *seen* to be etc. No point in heroics unless there's an audience.

'I thought you'd be pleased for us, Cass,' Dave said evenly.

'She is, Dave,' put in Simon.

I looked at him in amazement. It spoke! The spook spoke!

'It's just that she's tired. Hasn't taken the news on board properly, isn't that right, my dear?'

Was he some sort of minder? To our further amazement, the storm cloud passed from Cass's face. It was like watching two people in the one face. She brightened up, looked from Dave to Ragnell. 'You mustn't mind me,' she said. 'Simon is right. He knows what I'm like when I get tired, slows my reactions and all that. Look, I'm really pleased for you both. I hope you'll be so happy.'

A whole kitchenful of people heaved a sigh of relief. Crisis over.

'And you have no ring yet?' she continued, reaching out to take Ragnell's left hand. 'But you must get a ring. You must get this young lady the very best ring, Dave.'

Even Dave was taken aback by Cass's sudden change. She laughed an old woman sort of laugh.

'Thank you, Cass,' Ragnell said graciously.

'Listen,' Cass went on. 'Why don't the two of you go to Dublin and get that ring? How can you have an engagement without a ring?'

'Why Dublin?' exclaimed Ragnell. 'Bit far, isn't it?

Galway is nearer. Good jewellers in Galway...'

Dave laughed. 'She's right, you know, my old aunt,' he said. 'Let's do it. Tell you what, we'll fly to Dublin. How about that? We'll go on closing day, so you won't have to worry about the shop.'

Now I was caught up in the scene. This was more like it. 'Oh, do, Ragnell,' I enthused. 'It'd be deadly. How could you not?'

The boys were nodding. You could see they hadn't quite caught up with the emotional changes. Women are better at that sort of thing – jumping from one emotion to the other, I mean. Like Cass. It takes one woman to understand another.

So it was agreed. Ragnell was bossed by all of us into flying to Dublin with Dave to buy her ring. I nearly passed out with the excitement of it all. We drank tea and got excited again. Then Ragnell made a big thing of looking at her watch and suggested that we ought to be leaving. Dave led us down the hall. I thought he would strangle Leo for squealing and was looking forward to the prospect, but he waved down the kid's apologies.

'She had to be told sooner or later,' he said.

'And Simon too,' I said.

Always looking after the underdog, that's the type I am.

11

The Indian

That night we were in my room again, Jamie, Leo and I. You'd imagine Leo would have been suitably repentant and grovelly for being the cause of all the upset, but he seemed to be thrilled by the result of his clanger.

'You moron,' I said. 'Look at the trouble you almost caused, you and your big mouth.'

'Dave said it was OK,' he replied. 'He said that she had to be told anyway and that he was glad that we were all there. You heard him, isn't that right, Jamie?'

Jamie shrugged. 'What's said is said,' he muttered. 'It all turned out fine in the end.' He looked across at me. 'You're looking very thoughtful, Maeve. Is it about what Leo said?'

'Hm? No, just a nagging thought. It's nothing.'

'Come on,' encouraged Jamie. 'We'll un-nag it for you. What is it?'

I shifted about on the bed, not quite sure whether my nagging thought was worth mentioning. Oh well, maybe Jamie was right, maybe sharing it would un-nag it.

'It was a photograph I was looking at,' I began. 'An old photo of a group of cowboys...'

I broke off as Leo gave a loud guffaw. 'Cowboys! Come off it, Maeve. There's no such thing.'

'Well, for your information, smartass, there certainly is – or was. Dave's ancestor, the one who built that monstrosity of a house, made his money as a cowboy who drove cattle along the Goodnight Trail – that's where the house gets it strange name. Anyway, this photo was of a

78

group of guys in cowboy gear. One of them was the ancestor, I recognised him from another photo. But there was an Indian in the group – high hat with a feather and two pigtails.'

'What about him?' asked Leo as I hesitated.

I frowned and shook my head. 'There was something about him. Like, I felt I should know him. Do you believe in reincarnation?' I asked Jamie. 'Have you ever met someone and thought you'd met them before, like in a previous existence?'

'*Deja-vu*, it's called.' Trust Jamie to know. 'Happens to people all the time. A person or a place can give you an eerie feeling of familiarity. It has happened to me, yeah. But when you work it out there's usually an explanation. Nothing weird.'

'But why should I get that "*did ya view*" thing over a faded photo of a dead Indian?'

'Maybe you were his squaw in a previous life,' said Leo. Then he put his hand to his mouth and did some war-whoops. 'Keep clear, Jamie. Her old scalpum skills might come back.'

'Shut up, twit,' I said. 'That's offensive to ethnic people, that sort of carry-on.' I turned back to Jamie. 'It gave me the creeps, that photo.'

Jamie smiled. 'Don't worry about it. You probably mixed it up with some old Western movie with an Indian in it. A black and white movie, perhaps. That would do it. A black and white movie that you saw on telly as young kid and the image is back in the hard disc in your mind.'

'You're probably right,' I agreed. How was it that most things Jamie said made sense?

We talked some more and then watched *Friends* on the telly that Ragnell had thoughtfully left in my room. It was a repeat, but we had a laugh anyway. Afterwards Leo suggested another game of Monopoly. I promptly knocked that idea on the head.

'Afraid you'd have to make another big payout,' scoffed Leo.

I felt a jolt, a half-baked message trying to make sense in my half-functioning brain. 'What did you say?' I asked, peering intensely at Leo.

He backed away with mock terror. 'Don't scalp me, missus squaw-lady.'

'Stop messing. What did you say?'

Now Leo's expression changed to a 'my-cousin-is-mad' one. 'I only suggested a cruddy game, for heaven's sake! Lay off, Maeve.'

'No,' I went on. 'What did you say after that?'

Leo frowned, shrugged and looked at Jamie for confirmation that I was going doolally.

'He said something about you being afraid you'd have to make a big payout,' put in Jamie.

I leapt up. 'Payout!' I cried. 'That's it! Now everything is clear. I wasn't imagining it. This is … this is only bloody amazing!'

By now Leo had distanced himself from me, moved towards Jamie. Both of them looked at me as if I'd really and truly lost my marbles. But it wasn't that at all. In fact you could say I'd found my marbles.

'Payout,' I went on. 'That was the word, or something like it, that Charlie muttered when he saw the fan hanging in the shop.'

'So?' said Leo. 'Where's the big deal?'

'This deal,' I cried, so excited that the words were crowding to get out. 'That's who that Indian in the photo reminded me of – Charlie!'

'Oh, come off it, Maeve,' said Jamie. 'You're not still

on about that Indian. I told you...'

'No, it's true. That Indian was the total image of Charlie. No wonder I was struck by that photo. I'm telling you, it could have been Charlie looking out at me. Please, you've got to believe me. I'd ... I'd love to go back up to that house right now and prove it to you. It was when you said the word "payout" that triggered my memory, Leo. What could he have meant by that?'

'So, you reckon Charlie must be descended from this guy in the photo?' asked Jamie.

I nodded. 'Too much of a coincidence, him coming here. There's something weird about all this.'

'And he was looking for the Carstairs grave that day we met him,' added Leo, settling back on the bed now that he knew I was not a murdering lunatic. 'James Aloysius Carstairs.'

Now my head was completely on overdrive. 'That's it!' I spluttered. 'Old man Carstairs was known as JA! Dave told me so. I even saw his scrawly signature on another photo.'

'Wow!' said Leo. 'Spooky or what!'

'Could it be that Charlie is some way related to Dave?' I wondered aloud.

Jamie frowned. 'Not if his ancestor was in the same photo as Dave's,' he said. 'Two different ancestors, see?'

'So what's the connection? And how does the fan he so badly wanted come into it?' I asked

'The fan he's nicked,' added Leo. 'Don't forget he broke in...'

'But how did he break in?' I asked, defensively. 'The gardai said...'

'The key, remember? He must have lifted the key of the shop from Dave's jacket. Could have seen Dave let himself in earlier in the evening.'

'He's right,' agreed Jamie. 'The plot thickens, as they say in the best whodunits. Now we have several bits of information floating around, but how do we make a connection?'

We were stumped at that. Then Leo came up with one of his infrequent bright ideas.

'Let's log into North American Indians on the net,' he said, leaping from the bed. 'We might be lucky.'

Jamie nodded. 'Can't do any harm,' he said. So we beat it down the stairs to Ragnell's office.

'What are you three up to?' she called from the sitting-room, turning down the sound on the telly. 'Thought you'd gone to bed.'

'At this hour!' scoffed Leo. 'It's only a quarter past eleven. Do you think we're little kids or what? Can we have a go at the net?'

'Please,' I hissed. 'Say please. Don't you know how to win people over, you twit.'

'Please,' Leo added loudly.

'Suppose so,' said Ragnell, turning up the telly again.

We nearly tripped over one another in our eagerness to push into the small office. The iMac was only at 'sleep' so it didn't take long to start up. With the fingers of an expert, Leo logged into the search engine for Native Americans. Lots of stuff came up, but nothing that told us anything of use to our queries.

'Try crafts,' suggested Jamie.

A whole list of things came up under that; pottery, beadwork and things like that.

And then we all exclaimed together, 'Fans!'

'Go into "fans", Leo,' said Jamie, pointing to the menu. We leaned closer as we waited for the images.

'Chippewa Men's Decorative Fans,' I read. 'Made from birchbark.' But then Leo put up 'Flat Fans of the

Plains Region.'

We gasped when the image came on screen. It was exactly like the fan that had been nicked. Jamie read out the short note: *A contemporary fan made by the Native Americans of the plains consists of five to seven feathers which are individually decorated into a wooden handle.*

'Good grief!'

'Just like Dave's,' said Leo.

Jamie read on: *The handle is wrapped with leather and embellished with beaded applique with peyote beadwork.*

'What was that last bit again?' I interrupted.

'*Peyote beadwork...*'

'That's it!' I cried. '*Peyote*'. That's the word that Charlie muttered – the one that sounded like "payout". God, this is totally unreal! Go on.'

Peyote fans, or those associated with the religious rites of the Native Americans, are very serious and should not be copied, displayed, or treated disrespectfully.

Wow! That certainly set us thinking. None of us said anything; we just stared at the screen in amazement.

'No wonder Charlie wanted to get his hands on it,'

Jamie murmured eventually. 'Sacred to his people.'

'This is weird,' said Leo.

'Nothing weird about it,' I put in. 'He must have got one hell of a jolt when he saw the precious fan hanging from the ceiling.'

'And couldn't get you to sell it to him next day,' added Jamie.

'If only I'd known,' I muttered. 'I'd have given it to him, save him having to go and nick it. This is a right mess. What do we do now?'

Jamie looked thoughtful. 'I think maybe we should talk to Dave,' he said. 'After all it was his fan.'

'Yeah, but where did it come from?' I asked.

Jamie shrugged. 'That's not our concern. What we need to do is explain things to Dave. Maybe he won't be so upset when he knows the reason behind the theft.'

'It was still breaking and entering,' said Leo.

'Leave off with your "breaking and entering",' I scoffed. 'Can't you see that the man had to have this sacred fan. Though, I'm sure if he'd explained it to Ragnell and Dave they'd have gladly given it to him.'

'That's the point,' said Leo, with a note of triumph. 'Why do it the hard way? Why not talk?'

'He's right,' Jamie said. 'It's still a bit fishy.'

'He probably thought they wouldn't part with it,' I said. 'Here he is in a foreign country among people he doesn't know, and he has to make a snap decision. In his place I'd have done the same.'

'Except that you'd have got caught,' laughed Leo.

'Oh, give over,' I muttered. 'Look, Jamie's right, we'll nip over to Dave's in the morning and see what he has to say. With a bit of luck he'll tell the gardai not to make any more enquiries about the break-in and that'll be the end of it.'

'Anyway, that fan is probably winging its way back to the US as we speak,' said Jamie.

I had a mixture of feelings about that. I was dead sorry I wouldn't be seeing Charlie again – especially now that I knew he had an exotic background. I'd have fancied a visit with him to the American plains – wherever they were – to meet his people and be made a fuss of because I'd found their sacred fan. On the other hand I was glad he was safe from the condemnation of some grim-faced judge who'd clap him in the slammer. I felt very grown-up and mature in accepting that romance must take second place in the face of disaster. Sure, I'd mourn not having got to know Charlie better, but I could dream about what might have been. That's the sort of thing that makes a poet really great.

12

The Plane

We looked warningly at one another over breakfast next morning, willing each other not to let slip our discovery of the night before. There was no point in saying anything to Ragnell until we'd discussed it with Dave. At first I'd taken this as a bit sexist – and said so.

'Just because she's a woman,' I'd protested. 'Let the little woman stew while we discuss it with the big macho man. I don't think so!'

'It's not like that, Maeve,' Jamie had protested. 'But she's probably still feeling the sting of being broken into. Let her get herself together. Dave will know what to do and it will all work out, you'll see.'

And so, here we were, passing the cornflakes very politely with secret glances of conspiracy.

'We're just nipping out to show Jamie around,' I said, as we cleared up after breakfast. 'Will you manage all right on your own for a while, Ragnell?'

Ragnell laughed as she lifted her cup for Leo to wipe the table. 'I don't expect to be run off my feet. In fact it'll be a miracle if I sell so much as a painted pebble.'

'Don't be like that,' said Leo. 'It takes a while for a business to build up, Jim says so.'

'And what about all those people who were here at the official opening?' I went on encouragingly.

'Freeloaders,' muttered Ragnell. 'You'll always get the chattering masses to come to wherever there's booze and grub. When it comes to spending money they'll head for Galway or Dublin.'

'Oh, Ragnell, don't say that,' I pleaded. This sort of talk didn't fit in with her cool image. How could I attach myself to a role model who was sinking into defeat? Even if she was right.

Ragnell gave a wry smile. 'Don't mind me. I'm just in bad humour, feel like a bit of a moan.'

'Is it the break-in?' asked Leo. 'Has that put you in bad humour?'

Jamie and I gave him a meaningful look and he clamped the mouth shut.

'Partly,' sighed Ragnell. 'It's pretty gruesome to think that someone's been poking around without your knowing. Makes you feel soiled.'

'Well, at least the only thing taken was that old fan,' said Leo, eyeing Jamie and me warily in case we'd think he was going to spill the beans. Which is what we did think, of course. Now was not the time to get into a big discussion about that fan and all the baggage that went with it. Not before talking to Dave.

Ragnell gave another sigh. 'I'm having the locks changed today,' she said. 'Don't want some joker putting me through this again.'

I bit my lip, Jamie and Leo looked blank.

'Look, go on out, you lot,' went on Ragnell. 'I'll have my head sorted by the time you come back.'

'We'll do the afternoon,' I said. 'You can ... you can lie down or something.'

Ragnell smiled. 'Oh, Maeve. I'm not some old fogey needing to be humoured. But yes, I'll take up your offer for the afternoon. Now go, before I really do become an old fogey.'

Well, that sort of put a damper on the start of the day. We trudged up to Goodnight House, trying to be optimistic. 'Dave will sort all this,' Leo said.

'What's to sort?' asked Jamie, with the air of one not expecting an answer. 'The fan is gone, Charlie is gone. If that was all, it wouldn't matter too much – even if he did break in to take it.'

'What do you mean?' I asked.

'Well, there must be something deeper than all that,' went on Jamie. 'Charlie mooching about the Carstairs grave for one. What was he after? And then there's that photo you said you saw.'

'What do you mean "said" I saw?' I bristled. 'Do you not believe me? I'll show you when we get to the house. I'll show you that Indian who's a dead ringer for Charlie. Anyway, like you said, Charlie's gone. All we have to do is convince Dave to call off the gardai. And that'll be the end of it.'

But I suppose we should have known even then that it wasn't quite so simple.

It was Simon who answered the door when we rang. If he was surprised to see us it didn't register on his ex-pressionless face. With barely a word he showed us into the big sitting-room and went to get Dave.

I rushed straight to the table where the photos were arrayed.

'It's not here!' I exclaimed.

'Huh?' Jamie and Leo joined me.

'That photo, it's missing.'

All the other photos were there, including others of groups of cattle-drivers in cowboy gear, but there was no sign of the one with the Indian.

'Could it have slipped down behind the curtain?' asked Leo, stooping to check the gap between the table and the window. But there was no sign of it.

'Are you sure...?' began Jamie.

My laser look put paid to that question.

'Sshh,' put in Leo. 'Someone's coming.'

We swung around and tried to look innocent as Simon came back.

'He's not here, but the jeep is around the back so he's out on the land somewhere,' he said.

'Well, maybe we'll just have a look around outside for him,' Jamie said ever so politely.

'Was there something in particular you wanted to see him about?' asked Simon. 'Is it a message from the lady with the shop? Your aunt?'

The way he said that made it sound as if having a shop was way down the social scale.

'Ragnell, you mean,' I said. 'No. We just wanted to see Dave. He's fun.' Not like you, you spook, I felt like adding.

He followed us as we trooped to the front door.

'Making sure we don't dip into the family silver,' I whispered as we made our way across the drive. 'What is that guy? Is he some sort of butler? Poor relation? Or maybe he's Cass's lover-boy – though that image doesn't bear thinking about. Can you imagine those two wrinkly stick-insects snogging!'

'Probably just an old friend,' said Jamie. 'Didn't Dave say that he worked in Cass's business? Maybe he just had no place else to go and she invited him back with her.'

That sounded more plausible, but I preferred to think of him as a secret lover – after all, if two old fogies like them could find love, it gave hope to younger and prettier people. Like me.

We followed the drive and eventually came to a flat area with a landing-strip. The boys, of course, turned into gabbling idiots at the sight of the hangar and raced the rest of the way there.

Dave was inside messing about with spanners and rags

with oily hands. He was surprised to see us, and delighted because that's the kind he was.

'Figured you'd find your way here sooner or later,' he laughed. 'Come to meet my baby?'

'Your what?' said Leo.

'My baby. My Cessna 172. Great little plane.' He patted the side of the plane affectionately. 'Reliable and obedient, just like a woman,' he added, glancing at me with eyes glinting. I knew he was sending me up and I knew the boys were waiting for me to react. And I knew I shouldn't respond. And still I did.

'You're all the same, aren't you?' I said. 'Always have to be putting down women. Afraid of your pathetic little lives of the competition. Afraid you'll be outclassed at everything – and you are. Anyone could fly this thing. You lot should have been around when Dame Nellie Melba chained herself to the railings all those years ago when women were fighting for equality…'

'Hold on there, lady,' laughed Dave. 'No need to declare war, I was just kidding. And yes, of course a woman could fly this. Even Cass takes the controls now and then. Come on, Maeve, lighten up. Shouldn't respond to laddish teasing. I'd have thought a street-cred girl like you would know that.'

I scowled at the boys, trying to swallow the compliment, or at least trying to work out if it was one. Leo had a big, satisfied grin right across his ugly puss. That was to be expected, of course. I'd reacted just the way blokes liked.

I sniffed in a superior manner and glanced at Jamie. But he was more interested in the plane. He climbed aboard and oohed and aahed like a two year-old in a jelly-bean factory. Then all three of them got immersed in the workings of the plane. Well, it had four seats, lots

of dials and knobs, two wings, a few wheels, two engines – a right and a left. And that's all anyone needs to know about a plane. It goes up and, with a bit of luck, it comes down softly. But Dave was in his element showing us every nut and bolt. Boring.

I wandered out of the hangar to cool down and give out to myself for being so predictably prickly. Must be Ragnell's bad humour passing on to me, I thought. Or just the whole Charlie business. Okay, I know I made it clear that I fancied Jamie. No doubt about that, but it was in a real-life sort of way, if you know what I mean. With Charlie it was different. It was this romantic fantasy built around an older man with a ponytail and colourful roots – ethnic roots, I mean, not hair roots. With Charlie I could imagine a life deadly exotic and far removed from my ordinary life. The ideal, I had worked out, was to have a real-life boy for the realness of life, and a handsome foreigner to fantasise and drool over. But it's hard to drool over someone who'd led you to believe he was God's gift, only to go and nick your cousin's half-aunt's fiancé's fan. No wonder I was tetchy. Then I realised that Charlie was the whole reason we were here.

I went back inside.

'Maeve, Dave's going to fly us to Belfast when he comes back from Dublin.' Leo's face was flushed like a glow-in-the-dark monster-sticker. 'And he's going to give me a go at the controls.'

'Like hell I am,' put in Dave. 'I said I'd show you how they work, kid. Different ball game.'

Well, that was a relief. Being stuck up in the air in a small metal lunch-box with Leo at the controls is not the stuff of one's dreams.

'That'll be great,' I said with as much goodwill as I could muster to try and cancel my earlier tetchiness. Dave washed his hands with some foul-smelling green stuff and put on the kettle.

'Everyone for a cuppa?' he asked, putting out four mugs. 'No sugar, I'm afraid. I don't use it so I never think to have any here.'

I smelt mine before drinking, as you would in a place where oily things and bits of machinery predominate.

'About Charlie,' I began when there was a lull in the aerodynamics conversation.

'Charlie?' Dave looked puzzled.

'That's right,' added Leo. 'He was at the opening the other night. Me and Maeve met him in the graveyard looking for his family.'

'Bit late to come looking for family when they're at the graveyard stage, isn't it?' laughed Dave. His laugh faded when he saw that we were serious. And so we told him the whole story about Charlie.

When we'd finished, Dave looked from one to the other of us. 'And you reckon he was the one who stole the fan?'

'Who else?' shrugged Jamie.

'But he's gone now,' I said. 'He's on his way back to America, returning it to its proper place among his people.'

Dave tapped his mouth in a thoughtful sort of way. We said nothing while he mused.

'I'll have to inform the gardai,' he said eventually. 'It's already been reported so I'll have to tell them what you've told me. Even if it *is* a sacred thing,' he went on as I started to say something, 'it's still a case of breaking and entering. Look, I'll just finish off here and take you lot home. Then I'll go on to the garda station.'

'We could come too,' I said. I wanted to be on hand as a sort of defence. But Dave shook his head.

'Leave it to me,' he said. 'One voice is best.'

'Will you ask them to call off the search?' I went on.

'It'll be up to them,' replied Dave. 'The law is a funny thing. If they choose to pursue it, then that's up to them. Though I expect they'll let the matter drop if your man is already back in the States.'

I breathed a sigh of relief, which didn't go unnoticed. Leo gave me an exaggerated moony-eyed look and made a kissy mouth. Prat. However, I was so pleased that Charlie was probably going to get away with his sort of honourable theft that I zipped the lip.

I waited patiently while Dave did a bit more tinkering at the plane in preparation for the trip to Dublin tomorrow, avidly watched by the boys. I know that sounds really sexist, that I should have been stuck in there in the thick of nuts and rudders and all that, but a poet's got to do what a poet's got to do. You wouldn't have found Christina Rossetti stuck under a plane.

THE GREAT ESCAPE

By Maeve Morris

'My people need this sacred fan,'
Cried the rugged and handsome man.
And so he risked his life and limb.
No stint in jail would worry him.
Policemen chased him overseas,
Buzzed abroad like big blue bees.
But could they catch the clever thief?
Like hell they could! To my relief.
And though I've lost him, brave and bold,
I'll put my passionate love on hold.

Finally Dave gave the plane a pat on the belly. 'All set,' he said. 'Ready for take-off tomorrow.'

'And we'll look after everything,' I said, with all the maturity of a mother hen as we got into the jeep. 'You won't have to worry about a thing.'

'What?' said Dave, glancing at me in the mirror with mock horror. 'No afternoon rave parties? No wild discos? What a bunch of wimps.'

The boys and I looked at one another in shock. Until we realised Dave was winding us up. He knew full well that we didn't know anyone to invite to a rave, even if we did have one. He laughed at our shocked faces. 'Got you going there, didn't I?'

'No,' I replied, dead serious. 'But thanks for the idea. We'll work on it.'

I nudged Leo, who was sitting with me in the back. Jamie was in front with Dave. 'That'll shake him up.'

'Yeah,' giggled Leo. 'Just like Nellie Melba.'

'What's that supposed to mean?' I hissed. 'What has feminism got to do with it?'

'Oh, nothing,' muttered Leo. But I knew by his face that he was harbouring something evil. So I pinched him. 'Spill it out,' I hissed again.

'Ouch!' He rubbed his leg. 'That Nellie Melba you were on about, she was an opera singer,' he whispered harshly. 'You're mixing her up with a woman called Pankhurst...'

'Emmeline Pankhurst,' put in Jamie, twisting around. 'Went on hunger-strike to get votes for women.'

I glared at Leo. He nodded. 'True,' he said.

God, I'd done it again! My face must have been a pathetic mess – it certainly felt as if a hippo with attitude had walked right over it – because Jamie added, 'Easy to mix up the names. They kind of sound the same.'

But that didn't bring any consolation.

'I knew that,' I lied. 'Just testing.'

'She had a dessert called after her,' put in Dave.

'Who had?' asked Leo.

'Nellie Melba. Peach Melba is called after her.'

I swore never to look a peach in the face again. That was peaches and lemons off the list.

However all that embarrassment fled as we were driving up Main Street. I couldn't believe it when I saw a familiar figure going into the hotel.

'It's Charlie!' I exclaimed, glad and horrified all at once.

'So it is,' said Jamie, as we drove past.

'Shouldn't we go back?' said Leo. 'Have it out with him, tell him we know what he did?'

Dave shook his head. 'Not our place to do that,' he said. 'It's out of our hands. I'll do what I said, I'll report to the gardai.'

'Do … do you have to?' I muttered.

Dave looked at me in the mirror again and nodded. 'Afraid so. It's the right thing to do. The gardai will take it from there.'

I had aged a load of years by the time I dragged myself from the jeep at the shop. Dave warned us to say nothing to Ragnell, not to upset her. She'd only worry until charges were pressed, he said. He'd pick her up after he'd been to the garda station. Well, I was worried too.

'Your fault, all this.' I cornered Leo.

'Me? You're mad. How is it my fault?'

'You asked Charlie to the opening. If you hadn't done that, then he'd never have known about that fan.'

'I asked him because I saw that you were looking at him like a … like a dog looking at a bone.'

'Don't you call me a dog,' I said. Then I patted his chest when Jamie appeared. 'Just fixing Leo's tee-shirt,' I explained. 'It's a cousin thing.'

Leo scowled and wrenched himself away from my grasp. Jamie looked puzzled, but thought better of asking any questions.

'Was that Dave's jeep I heard?' asked Ragnell, coming into the shop from the back. 'Isn't he coming in?'

'He's gone to the s……' began Leo.

'He's got something to do in town,' said quick-thinking Jamie. 'He'll be back soon.'

'I was going to say *supermarket*,' muttered Leo when Ragnell was momentarily out of earshot. 'Do you take me for a total prat?'

There was a lot of mixed-up thinking going on in my brain and I didn't like any of it. Why did that stupid Charlie have to come back? Why didn't he just take his fan and do a runner, like any decent thief? Now there'd be all kinds of trouble for him. Dave was probably, right this minute, yakking to the gardai. And they'd be sending the posse out for Charlie. I felt sick – a falling-over-a-cliff sort of sick.

'I'm going to my room,' I announced, hand to head in a beautiful pose. 'I'll be fine in a little while.'

As if anyone was interested. The boys were telling Ragnell about the plane. The three of them looked at me.

'Would you like a Panadol or something?' asked Ragnell.

I shook my head. 'I'll be OK. You go on out with Dave when he comes back. The boys will take care of the shop until I come down. I'll only need half an hour or so.' And, with the convincing grace of a wonderful martyr, I closed the door between the shop and the house, listened for a while while they went on about the plane, and let myself gently out by the front door.

13

Things get Really Serious

At least I didn't have to ask for Charlie at reception; he was sitting at a table in the lobby, just about to dig into a plate of sandwiches. The nerve of the man! He looked up when he saw me coming and gave me a wave and a grin as if he was the most innocent creature in the world.

'What did you come back for?' I asked, sitting opposite him. 'Didn't you know you'd be rumbled?'

He stopped, a soggy salad sandwich half-way to his mouth. 'Excuse me?' he said.

'The fan,' I prompted.

His face took on the sort of expression you'd have yourself when you'd say, 'What homework, miss?'

'What about the fan?' he said evenly.

'Well,' I went on patiently. 'I'd have thought you'd make yourself scarce after nicking it. What made you come back?'

Charlie put down the half-eaten sandwich.

'The fan has gone?' he asked.

Nice one, I thought. But he had no need to come the innocent with Maeve. I gave a sort of snort, which is not a very clever thing to do unless your nostrils are dry. As I wiped my nose with a rather tatty tissue, Charlie twined his fingers together and leaned closer.

'Go on,' he said. 'Tell me more.'

'I was hoping you'd be the one telling me...' I began.

But Charlie waved away my words. 'I want to hear it from you first,' he said.

Well, that seemed a bit strange, me telling a thief

about his own theft, but if that was the way to get an explanation, then so be it. So I told him how we'd seen him leaving the hotel on the night of the theft, the break-in from the inside (forgetting to ask him how he got hold of Dave's keys) and how we'd found out all that stuff on the net about the fan and its value to his people. I even told him about the photo of his ancestor up at Goodnight House. That fairly shook his bones. His face grew tight and thoughtful.

'He *is* your ancestor, that Indian, isn't he?' I said. 'So what have you to say?'

Charlie took a deep breath. 'Look,' he said, with an air of resignation. 'I know what you must be thinking, but hear me out. I'll tell you the whole...'

He broke off as two figures suddenly materialised beside us.

'Mr Knight?' said one of the men. Charlie nodded. 'We'd like to ask you a few questions,' the man went on.

'And you are?' asked Charlie, calm as you like. The men produced badges, like you'd see in *Frost* or any of those police dramas that Mam watches. Charlie nodded. 'How can I help you?' he said. I marvelled at his nerve. Me, I'd have been clawing my way up the curtains.

The men looked at me; I took it that was my cue to leave. But not before hearing one of the gardai ask Charlie for his passport. As I was crossing the lobby, I heard the garda say, 'But this is not the name you've given to hotel reception.'

I didn't wait for Charlie's reply. I was too shocked. There was me thinking there might be some redemption for Charlie, especially when he'd been about to tell me the full story. With a hard rock thumping where my heart should be, I went back to Ragnell's place. The two boys were in the shop. And nobody else. Bad craft day.

'Are you feeling better, Maeve?' asked Jamie. 'You look like someone whose pet monkey's been picked for space experiments.'

'Worse,' I mumbled. 'I've just been to see Charlie.'

'You what!' exclaimed Leo. 'You big nellie. You've warned him off.'

'Too late for that,' I said. So I told them about my meeting with Charlie, word for word.

'So he's even been using a false name?' said Jamie when I'd finished. I nodded miserably. 'Well then,' went on Jamie. 'It doesn't look good, does it? People only use false names when they're up to no good, have something to hide.'

'But he was going to tell me,' I protested feebly. 'He was going to explain it all to me. Trust the fuzz to turn up at the wrong moment.'

'What's there to explain, Maeve?' said Leo. 'Like Jamie says, it doesn't look good. Better not say anything to Dave about this. Wouldn't want him to think you were aiding and abetting a crime.'

'You make it sound like Charlie's some kind of psychopath or something,' I retorted. 'It was only an old fan, for heaven's sake.'

'It was still a criminal thing,' said Jamie. He said it gently, but whether that was to save my feelings or stop me from throwing a mad tantrum I don't know. But I knew defeat when I met it. There was no explaining away Charlie's actions. My whole body just drooped down to my shoes.

Leo, however, was far from droopy. His face was beaming and he looked like he was going to burst.

'Guess what?' he said.

'You're going to tell me anyway, aren't you?' I replied.

'I'm going with Dave and Ragnell tomorrow,' he said,

his voice up several decibels with the excitement. 'Dave was here just a while ago and said I could go. Isn't that deadly?'

I looked at Jamie. 'How about you?' I asked. 'You going too?'

Jamie shook his head. 'No. I'll wait till we're all going.'

I turned back to Leo. 'You mean you're going on this romantic trip for an engagement ring? You're going to muscle in on…'

I broke off. Hold everything there, Maeve, my brain was saying. If Leo was going with Dave and Ragnell, then that meant that there'd be just Jamie and me. A whole day to ourselves, like that regular date that I'd wished for. A whole day! Suddenly my body began to undroop. The grey cloud over my head changed to psychedelic fireworks. For the first time ever we'd be rid of Leo the Dancing Flea, me and Jamie, and be able to talk about deep and meaningful things befitting our superior status. Blessings on the head of the inventor of Cessnas and all flying metal things. I smiled at Jamie, and he nodded, raising his eyebrows in an understanding gesture.

'Do you mind?' asked Leo.

'Huh?'

'Do you mind if I leave you two and go?'

Not on your great spotted knickers, I thought.

'Oh, we'll find things to do,' I said, trying very hard to play down my delight. 'Explore a bit, maybe.'

'You sure?' asked Leo. 'I mean, if you really wanted me to stay I wouldn't mind…'

'Liar,' I said. 'Your heart would sink to your knobbly knees. Look, don't go on about it or we might change our generous minds.' I paused to let him tell me how wonderful I was. As you would. Power. But did he grovel gratefully? Did he heck!

'I'll bring you home a Peach Melba,' said Leo.

'Don't push your luck, sunshine,' I growled. 'We could object that it wasn't fair and have you grounded.' As if. But the odd threat never goes astray.

We minded the shop, as we'd promised. Mind it? Except for one old bird who deliberated for ages over a platter for her grandaughter's wedding, we had the place to ourselves.

'Is it hand-thrown?' she asked.

Jamie saw my brain clicking into position for a beautiful reply and jumped in before I could say it.

'All this pottery is hand-thrown, Ma'am,' he said. Spoilsport. But his politeness won her over and she forked out for the platter.

'That should keep Ragnell in a life of luxury,' I said as I put the fifteen euros in the till.

'I told you,' said Leo. 'It takes a while to get a business going.'

'Like a bunch of lifetimes,' I replied. 'She'd be better of buying scratch cards with that big sale and take a chance of winning. What on earth possessed her to open a craft shop in a dive of a town like this? She must have been making a decent living before now.'

'She was teaching somewhere in England,' said Leo. 'She hated it. Nearly did her head in. When a bunch of scumbags nicked her car from the school yard she said that was the last straw and decided to come home.'

'Jeez, I didn't know that,' I said. 'And then she comes home and is broken into. No wonder she was in the grumps earlier.' I turned to Jamie. 'So that's what your schools are like over there?'

Jamie smiled. 'Not all of them,' he said.

'Not posh ones like yours,' I went on. 'All rugby and

cricket and jolly hockey sticks.'

'Whatever,' he said, a bit rattled.

Not to worry, I'd make it up to him tomorrow. Maybe I'd cook a candlelight meal and we'd finish one of those leftover bottles of wine. Totally grown-up. But then I remembered the last dinner I'd cooked at home and thought maybe not. Spaghetti Bolognese takes on a whole new meaning when the stringy bits get glued together in a lump.

We stayed in for the night. Ragnell got the video of *Chicken Run*. We hadn't the heart to tell her we'd seen the movie, and that we were a bit up the age scale for that sort of entertainment (although I always love Wallace and Grommit). But she meant well and, besides, she'd bought crisps and popcorn which compensated more than a bit. Especially when we stuffed popcorn into our cheeks to make Wallace and Grommit grins.

'Are you sure you two don't mind staying behind tomorrow, Maeve and Jamie?' Ragnell asked as we headed for bed. I thought about that for a few moments – just long enough for Leo to sweat and worry.

'We'll be fine, thanks,' replied Jamie. "We'll do the touristy thing and explore.'

Yeah, right on, Jamie.

I hugged myself as I snuggled into my bed. Tomorrow I was going on a real date.

14

A Real Date?

As we passed the hotel in Ragnell's car on our way to Goodnight House, I strained my neck to peer in, see if there was any sign of Charlie.

Jamie saw what I was at and gave a sort of sympathetic nod. But there was no sign of our Indian friend. If you could call someone who breaks into places, nicks stuff and gives a false name a friend. But some people are drawn to criminals and I was beginning to think I might be one of them. Maybe in a previous existence I'd been a gangster's moll. Better still – a gangster.

MACHINE-GUN MAEVE

By Maeve Morris

She terrorised the city streets
With flashy car and daring feats.
'Hand over all,' she waved her gun.
'I want your jewels and all your mon.'
She gambled hard, smoked fat cigars,
Drank gin and stuff in dodgy bars.
Though chased by cops, some wimps, some brave,
None ever caught Machine-Gun Maeve.

I wondered if Charlie was still being questioned. I tried not to picture him sitting in front of two gardai with a tape recorder, and him sweating and smoking and asking for a lawyer. My heart gave a lurch, but there was nothing I could do. I couldn't even talk to the boys about it because Ragnell wasn't to be told until everything was sorted. So I just pursed my lips and looked soulful.

'Why are you coming?' asked Leo, giving me a wary look. 'You and Jamie. Why are you coming?'

I could see that he was afraid I would change my mind and make a fuss. I gave a deep sigh. 'I don't know,' I began, 'I just can't decide.'

'Decide what?' The fear in Leo's voice was worth anything. I scratched my chin thoughtfully.

'Will it be Chinese or fish and chips for lunch?'

Leo's sigh of relief made me laugh. Don't you just love to create sweat in young cousins? We pulled up at the front door. There was no sign of either Cass or Simon.

'Here you are, Maeve,' said Ragnell, taking the keys out of the ignition and handing them to me.

'Why are you giving them to me, Ragnell?' I asked. 'We're not going to *drive* anywhere.'

Ragnell laughed. 'I know that. But the house keys are on the same ring. You'll be wanting to get in. There's food in the freezer, but don't eat too much.'

'OK,' I muttered. Did she think we were going to spend our valuable time stuffing our faces with grub?

Ragnell laughed again. 'I'm not being mean,' she said. 'It's just that we're booked into Chez George for seven o'clock. To celebrate the ring and all that,' she went on when she saw my gobsmacked expression.

'Oh, wow!' I said. 'All of us?'

'All of us.'

I didn't think to ask if that included Cass and Simon. But what the heck! I had a date with Jamie and nothing else mattered.

Dave was already at the plane.

'Come on, you lot,' he said. 'Before I chicken out of this trip and decide to stay a bachelor.'

'Fine,' said Ragnell with mock scorn. 'But you'll still have to take this child for a plane ride like you promised, so I might as well come too. Cheers,' she turned to wave to Jamie and me. 'We'll be home around half five or six.'

I couldn't wait for them to be off. It was only twelve o'clock and we were going to have until about six o'clock, Jamie and me. Nearly six uninterrupted hours of Jamie's company. And, as I watched the small aircraft build up speed and ease into the sky, I was very glad to be right here on the ground. We watched until it was just a speck in the sky, then Jamie turned to me.

'Want to go down to the river?' he asked.

'Don't mind,' I answered.

If he'd asked me to walk on water, I would. We walked back down the avenue towards the house. Now that my great longed-for moment had arrived, I was totally tongue-tied. All the scintillating conversations I'd often practised in the mirror for this very occasion just vanished. Not to worry, something would hit the brain sooner or later. And maybe I'd end up in Jamie's arms, so who'd need words then?

'This is nice,' said Jamie.

'What is?'

'Having the day to ourselves.'

'It is?' Cool, just like Ragnell.

'Yeah. I'm glad, aren't you?'

I took a deep breath to slow down my mouth before it could run away with words I'd regret.

'Mmm,' I said.

Jamie looked at me with surprise. 'If you'd prefer to do something else...' he began. 'I can...'

I gulped. This wasn't how it should be. Not a threat of splitting, no way!

'No, Jamie. I'm thrilled that we have this time together. I really, really am.' And so it all came out in a rush, how pleased I was that we were together, how I liked him such an amazing lot, how we'd never ever had time together, how I often thought of him during some boring class (and was told I had a low attention-span), how I wished he didn't live so far away...

'Sshh, Maeve,' he laughed, putting his finger on my lip. 'I didn't ask for a confession. Take it easy.'

For the second that his finger was on my lip I wondered if he could feel my pulse racing. Now I was red and embarrassed. My coolness had gone up into the air with Ragnell. Maeve the Mess ruled again. When would I get it right?

'I didn't mean all that,' I fibbed. 'It just sort of fell out of my mouth.'

'Yes you did,' laughed Jamie. 'But I like all you said. I really do, Maeve Morris.'

'You do? You don't think I'm, like, pushy?'

'No, I don't think you're pushy at all. I like you just the way you are.'

This was one of those moments that you'd like to freeze and take it out every now and again to savour. And we were going to have a whole day like this! Sometimes, I thought, life gets so sweet that your head can't take any more. We crossed the avenue near the house and went through the trees that led to the river. The sun shone through the trees, birds sang, grass swished softly. If an orchestra had suddenly materialised and a fairy god-mother appeared in a bubble, it would have been just right. But it was no fairy godmother who stepped out from the trees.

'Charlie!' I exclaimed. 'Charlie, is that you?'

And so it was. No mistaking that square jaw and pony-tail. 'What are you doing here?'

Charlie looked behind us to make sure we were on our own. Then he beckoned to us to follow him into the trees. Jamie and I looked at one another with surprise and went after him.

'Are you on your own?' he asked. 'Anyone following on to join you?'

'No, there's just us,' said Jamie. 'Why are you here? We thought…'

'… you were in trouble with the gardai,' I finished.

Charlie fixed steely eyes on me. 'Was it you put them on to me?'

I shifted about from one foot to the other. 'Well, there was that fan,' I began. 'You were mad keen to get it. And then when it was nicked…'

'You immediately assumed it was me.'

'What else could we think?' I said defensively. 'We saw you that night, just before the break-in, we saw you leave the hotel with your bag. Next thing we know Ragnell's been broken into and the fan is gone and you're gone. Nobody else was interested in that old thing.'

'That "old thing" as you call it,' said Charlie, now with steel in his voice, 'is very precious to my people.'

'Yes, we know that, Charlie,' said Jamie.

'You do?' Charlie's expression turned to surprise.

'I told you. We looked it up on the net,' I said. 'We found out about your peyote fan and how important it is to your people. That's what clinched our suspicion. You were the only one who could want it. So, what have you to say to that, eh? There was no need to break in...'

'I didn't break in,' Charlie interrupted. 'It wasn't me.'

'Come on,' I said, all my Charlie fantasies spluttering into extinction like a burnt-out candle. 'Don't try that on us. You even changed your name, for heaven's sake. I heard those two cops say it when they looked at your passport. Why change your name and then expect us to believe you when you act the innocent?'

Charlie made a sort of helpless gesture with his hands. 'I'm telling you...' he began.

'And I'm telling you,' I cut across his words, 'we're not total eejits, you know...'

'Sshh, Maeve,' put in Jamie, putting his hand on my arm. 'Let him speak. Go on, Charlie.'

Charlie nodded gratefully. 'It's a long story,' he said, sitting on a tree stump.

'It would be, wouldn't it?' I said sarcastically. 'You've had plenty of time to make it up...'

'Maeve!' said Jamie sharply. 'Cut it out. Listen'.'

I scowled at Charlie and sat on another stump beside Jamie, giving him a good scowl too for good measure.

'Like I said,' Charlie said quietly. 'it's a long story.

15

Charlie's Story

We sat entranced, Jamie and me, while Charlie told us a tale which was unreal. To begin with he told us that his real name was Charlie Goodnight.

'Ah, the Goodnight Trail,' I said.

Charlie was surprised. 'That's right,' he said. 'For generations the first son in my family was called after Charles Goodnight, the cattle king who drove his cattle along the trail that he gave his name to. It was he who hired my ancestor, treated him and his family very fairly at a time when others were not so kind to Native Americans...'

'And took their land. Greedy racist pigs,' I said angrily. 'If I'd been there I'd have fought for the ethnic people...'

'Maeve,' said Jamie, 'shut up and listen. Please,' he added because he was polite. So I pressed my lips together and didn't open them again until Charlie was finished. This is how the story went.

During the eighteen sixties and seventies, when cattle driving was at its height, Charlie's ancestor worked the trail. Because of the long, arduous journey, a special bond would form between the cowboys. They'd camp together, talk around the camp fire at nights and look out for one another.

One of the frequent cattle-drivers who teamed up with Charlie's ancestor was called James Aloysius Carstairs – he of the granite face and curly whiskers in the photo. When they'd get to the end of a drive, the cowboys would head for the bath house and the saloon. Except, as Dave had already told me, Mr JA Carstairs. He used to stay in the camp, minding his money. The cowboys came to trust him, so much so that they'd leave part of their pay with him so that they wouldn't gamble it all away.

That was fine and dandy until old JA got greedy. One night, while the boys were whooping it up, he took their money and absconded. The men were furious, as you would be if the money you'd earned by sitting on a horse for days, fighting snakes, eating leathery food, and swallowing the dust of thousands of steers, was nicked by a holy Joe who'd abused their trust in him. Of course a search was made, but JA got clean away.

Charles Goodnight very decently gave the boys some of their losses back. 'Wanted' posters were put up in frontier towns for the capture of Carstairs, but time passed and he was forgotten. Except by Charlie's ancestor. However, what upset him most was the fact that the thieving git had taken his precious peyote fan – a sacred item that, as a chief, he carried with him everywhere. He was devastated.

The story of the theft of the fan was handed down to every generation. In the nineteen seventies, when Charlie was a small boy, his grandfather used to talk longingly of the sacred fan. He remembered Carstairs talked a lot about Ireland, the land of his parents' birth. He figured that that was where Carstairs had fled and he wished he had enough money to go there and reclaim it. Charlie promised him that, as soon as he could, he would do just that.

Charlie had gone to university, specialising in the history of his people. With access to all kinds of information, including records of the employment of people on the cattle trails, he looked up Carstairs and found his parents' emigrant records, and where they had come from. And now, with his grandfather dying, Charlie had booked in with a package tour to Ireland, intending to break off from the organised tours to try and locate the fan for his grandfather. That was how he happened to be in the graveyard on that day that Leo and I had met him; he had to establish that he was in the right place. You can imagine the shock he got when he came upon Goodnight House. *That* was why he gave a false name at the hotel; he didn't want to arouse suspicion. And why he had to shoot down Leo's suggestion that he was looking for the Carstairs link.

'You must have nearly fainted when you saw the fan hanging in Ragnell's shop,' I said. 'If only you'd said, if only I'd known, I'd have given it to you that time you offered me fifty euros for it.'

Charlie shrugged. 'I wasn't thinking straight,' he said. 'I didn't know who to trust.'

'Could've trusted me,' I sniffed. 'And where did you disappear to, that night we saw you?'

'Had to go to Dublin,' he replied. 'I got a lift with a sales rep who'd been staying in the hotel. I had to meet up with the tour operators, to prove I was still part of the group, even though I hadn't been on the tours with them. They can get shirty when people step out of line.'

'But, hang on,' put in Jamie, leaning towards Charlie. 'If you didn't take the fan, then who did?'

'Someone who knows the story,' said Charlie. 'Someone who thinks that I'll blow the whistle on the source of the Carstairs fortune.'

'And is that what you intend to do?' asked Jamie.

Charlie shook his head. 'Money is not the issue,' he said. 'For my grandfather's sake, I just want the fan.'

'But who would know why you were here?' said Jamie again. 'Who could possibly recognise you?'

I nearly wet my knickers in my mad rush to get the words out.

'That photo!' I spluttered. Jamie and Charlie looked at me. 'The one I told you about, Jamie, with the cowboys and the Indian...'

'Who you said looked just like Charlie,' finished Jamie, realisation dawning on him. 'And when you went to show it to Leo and me ..'

'It was gone!' I burst out. 'Someone had sussed that I was looking at it. Someone who knew I knew Charlie.'

'Someone who thinks I'm a threat to the Carstairs estate,' said Charlie.

'Dave?' said Jamie. 'Cass?'

'It was Dave who gave Ragnell the fan, remember,' I said.

Jamie nodded. 'Doesn't really mean anything. He could have figured it was safe in Ragnell's shop. The likelihood of anyone coming to this sleepy town in the middle of Ireland and recognising it is very small.'

'Oh, God, I hope it's not Dave,' I groaned. 'What with the engagement and all.'

'Cass?' said Jamie.

'The old lady?' Charlie shook his head. 'Unreal. Does she look the type to break in and steal?'

Something tried to surface from the back of my mind, like when you put something in water and it takes ages to come to the surface. And then, splash! there it was. 'That night...' I said.

'What night?'

I frowned, keeping the thought before it sank again. 'The night of the break-in. Dave said he was going to ring Simon to tell him to push the plane into the hangar,

remember? Because of the wind?' Jamie nodded doubt-
fully. 'He was away for ages,' I continued. 'And when he
came back, Ragnell asked him if he'd got through to
Simon...'

'And Dave said he hadn't, that he wasn't there,' said
Jamie. 'Jeez, Dave could have done it. Pretended his key
was missing afterwards.'

I felt my heart sink. How would we ever tell Ragnell
that she was engaged to the descendant of a thieving git
whose warped set of morals had passed on to her fiancé?
It didn't bear thinking about.

'Hold on a sec,' said Jamie.

'What?'

'Where was Simon?'

'Huh?'

'If Dave went to phone Simon and he wasn't there,
where was he at that hour of the night?'

'Oh cripes,' I groaned again. 'This is getting compli-
cated. You're saying now that Simon could be in on
this?'

And then I remembered the way Simon had looked at
me that time I was holding the photo in my hand. And
the way he watched us with his spooky eyes. Yes, that
made sense. A bit.

'Do you think they're in it together?' I asked.

'Look,' put in Charlie. 'Does it really matter who?
Thing is I've come a long way to get that fan. It was
almost in my grasp. Can you help me?'

Jamie shrugged. 'What can we do?'

'Help me to find it.'

'You mean nick it again?' I said. 'This is getting to be
the most nicked fan in the world.'

'It's not stealing if it's going back to its rightful
owners,' said Charlie, slightly sourly I thought.

'Where would we look?' I asked. 'In the house?'

Charlie nodded. 'In the house. I'm sure that's where it is. But I don't want you to get into trouble. All I ask is that you keep watch. The old lady and that guy you mentioned – Simon, is it? – they left about half an hour ago. I've been here for a few hours. If I could just get into the house I know I'd suss it out. It's the only chance I'll get. I couldn't bear to have come this far and have to return empty-handed to my grandfather.'

'But if you're caught?' I began.

Charlie gave a scornful laugh. 'Can't be in much more trouble than I am now.'

'What do you mean?' asked Jamie.

'They've held on to my passport, those two policeman. They're checking me out. I'm supposed to stay in the hotel, which is why I'm holed up here. No point in hanging around the hotel waiting for them to come back and see me out of town. They seem to be worried about illegal asylum-seekers or something. Look, if you'd rather not get involved I'll understand. But today is my only chance. My flight home is tomorrow.'

'Of course we'll help,' I said. 'Won't we, Jamie?'

Jamie nodded. 'No problem.'

'We'll come in and help you search,' I went on.

We went back to the house. Front door locked. We went around the back. Back door locked. We went around to the front again.

Charlie looked up at the balcony. 'There's a window open up there,' he said. With that he heaved himself on to the roof of the porch and, with the greatest of ease, leapt on to the balcony. Without a sound, he slipped through the open window. We waited for him to unlock the front door.

'Are we mad?' I whispered to Jamie.

'Probably,' he said.

'But I can't help thinking about that old grandfather dying without seeing his precious fan … What? Why are you looking at me like that?'

Jamie smiled. 'Don't get too soft, Maeve,' he said. 'We don't know who to trust, do we?'

'But … but why offer our help if you don't believe this guy?'

'Actually it was you who threw us into the deep end,' he said. 'Sshh, here he comes.'

Oh lord, what had I done, I wondered, as I stepped over the threshold. Would we end our so-called date in the clink, me and Jamie, for aiding a criminal? I felt like I was swimming in choppy water without water-wings.

We split up to start our search. Well, where do you start to look for a feathery fan in a vast house? Of course it was me, with my superior logic, who found the wretched thing. Sure, it was much later, but to cut a long story short, find it I did.

'Maeve, you're a marvel,' said Jamie when I called out. 'What on earth prompted you to look in the airing cupboard?'

'A hunch,' I said modestly. Not really. I always look into people's airing cupboards whenever I visit strange houses. My mother always said that you could gauge a lot about people by their airing cupboards, so I'd got into the habit since I was very young. Not that I ever learned anything about people by doing it, but old habits have a way of relieving monotony, and by then I'd given up on the old fan and was looking for diversion.

Not that I was ever going to admit that, you understand.

'Not alone that,' I said, 'but this was with it.'

'The photo!' exclaimed Jamie. 'The one with the Indian – Charlie's ancestor.'

Just then Charlie joined us. 'What is it?' he said. He nearly passed away when I handed him the fan. He held it reverently. 'After all these years,' he whispered. 'My people's peyote fan.'

'And this,' I said, handing him the photo. 'Surely that's your ancestor.'

Charlie looked at it and smiled. 'We have a copy of this at home,' he said. 'And yes, that is my great-great-grandfather.' He gave a huge sigh and looked at me with admiration, as he should.

But before I could glow in the light of my heroic deed, which only I knew wasn't heroic at all, we heard the crunch of tyres on the gravel outside.

Jamie ran to the window. 'It's them!' he exclaimed. 'Cass and Simon. What'll we do?'

'First rule in an emergency,' said Charlie calmly, 'is not to panic. Follow me. Remember the tracking we did the other day? Think like a shadow.'

We stayed behind him as he eased along the corridor. Every now and then he'd stop and listen, looking like a bird with head on one side. Maybe that was his Indian name, I thought, the way utterly weird stuff comes into your head when you least want it to. 'Come in for your tea, Bird-With-Head-On-One-Side, and stop drawing grafitti on the teepee.'

I smothered a hysterical giggle and Jamie looked at me and frowned. No, that wasn't a poetic frown either. More of a you're-a-mad-twit frown. Which only reminded me that we were supposed to be on a hot date. Some date this was turning out to be – following an Indian down the corridor of Leo's step-aunt's fiancé's house after nicking an already nicked feathery fan which had come from the Goodnight trail over a hundred and fifty years ago. Try explaining that to a hairy-wigged judge in court. It would be straight to the slammer for the three of us, and curtains for Charlie's old grandfather without seeing his fan.

Charlie held up his hand, head on one side again. 'They're at the back of the house,' he whispered. 'Probably putting away groceries in the kitchen.'

Then he waved us on again. We went downstairs without so much as a creak. At the bottom, Charlie listened again. Murmur of voices. Then he made a frantic signal for us to follow him through the open front door. We didn't stop until we were halfway up the hidden avenue that led to the hangar, out of sight of the house.

'Now what?' asked Jamie, panting.

'Lie low for a little while,' said Charlie. 'If we're found up at the hangar, at least you two have an excuse, that you were just chilling out after seeing the others off; I'll stay out of sight until it's safe to venture back. Maybe they'll go out again.'

'How did you know about the hangar?' asked Jamie, with a tad of suspicion.

'I've checked out every inch of this place,' replied Charlie. 'Remember my great-great-grandfather's money partly financed it.'

That thought certainly sobered us.

'We might as well have a cup of coffee,' I said as we went into the hangar. 'I'm gasping for a caffeine fix after all that stress. Anyone else?'

Jamie and Charlie nodded, Charlie concentrating on the fan he'd taken out from inside his jacket.

'And there's even some sugar,' I laughed, pointing to a bag on the floor. 'Dave must have changed his mind.'

'What do you mean?' asked Jamie, wiping out the mugs with a grimy tea-towel.

'Said he didn't take sugar, remember? Said he never kept sugar here.' I picked up the bag. 'Hell!' I exclaimed. 'It's empty. How could he have got through a whole bag of sugar since yesterday? Must be on a binge.'

Charlie looked up, a startled expression on his face. 'What are you saying?' he asked, putting the fan back inside his jacket.

'The sugar,' I laughed. 'When we were here yesterday, Charlie said that...'

'I heard that bit,' Charlie rudely interrupted. 'That bag – did you say it's empty?'

'Bloody is,' I replied, stung by his rudeness. 'Look, it doesn't matter...'

I broke off as Charlie grabbed Jamie. 'Show me where

the plane was standing,' he said. 'The exact spot.'

'What...?' began Jamie.

'The exact spot,' said Charlie, his face white and tense.

Now it all fell into place, I thought. We have a mad Indian on our hands. Fan me eye, this guy had broken out of some institution that had padded walls and men in white coats. Keep calm, Maeve, and always remember to bring your mobile in future in case you ever run into left-over cowboys with a grudge. If there was going to *be* a future.

I watched, dumbfounded as Charlie half-dragged Jamie outside. God, I'd be a widow before I'd even had my hot date! Jamie led Charlie to where the plane had been, and pointed, too shaken to speak. Charlie let him go and was down on his hands and knees, brushing the tarmac with his fingers. Jamie looked helplessly back at me. I tried to mouth the words 'run for it', but my mouth wasn't working very well. Suddenly Charlie stood up. His face was still white. White and thunderous.

'It's been sabotaged!' he shouted. 'The plane has been sabotaged. It's going to crash!'

16

Sabotage!

Charlie practically pushed Jamie back to the hangar. I was still standing with my mug of coffee in my hand, trying to make sense of Charlie's outburst. Sabotage? Crash?

'Where have they gone?'

Charlie still had a hold of Jamie's sweater. Jamie's face was going through every emotion that a face could register – fear, horror and amazement being the main ones.

'Dublin,' stammered Jamie, pulling himself free. 'Look, Charlie, what are you on about? We saw them off around midday, didn't we, Maeve?' I nodded, frozen to the spot. 'The plane took off fine,' he continued. 'There was no sabotage. I don't know what...'

'Sugar,' interrupted Charlie.

'Excuse me?'

'Sugar,' went on Charlie. 'Someone has put sugar into one of the tanks. If the plane took off all right, it means that the sugar is in the tank they'll use for the return journey. We have to stop them before they set out for home. Unless...'

He stopped, a look of horror on his face.

'Unless what?' I asked.

Charlie took a deep breath. 'Unless your friend switches the selector button from one tank to the other in mid-flight. He can do that if fuel is low.'

'Oh my God! What are you saying?' I whispered.

'I'm saying that those people are going to die unless

we can get the message to them that their plane has been interfered with.'

'What can we do?' asked Jamie, suddenly all business again.

'Head for the airport,' replied Charlie. 'We need to head for the airport. And we need to be able to communicate with airport security.' He wrung his hands in frustration. 'How can we do all that? Come on, think. Could we hire a car?'

'In this town?' I said. 'There isn't even a taxi.'

But then I remembered something. 'Ragnell's keys!' I cried, fishing them from the pocket of my jeans. 'Her car key is on the same ring as the door key. Car's parked outside the front door. Let's go.'

We sprinted down that avenue like rats in a cattery or cats in a doggery. There was a slight pause when we reached the car. Who was going to drive? Charlie looked perplexed.

'It has to be you,' I said, tossing him the keys. 'Jamie and I are under age.'

'Oh my gosh!' said Charlie as he settled behind the wheel. I hopped into the back – well it was probably the safest place to be, and besides Jamie would be more help to Charlie in navigating and all that.

'Everything's on the wrong side,' went on Charlie. 'And gears – I'm used to automatic.'

'Come on, it's easy,' said Jamie.

And, typical of Jamie, he had the rudiments of driving the Nissan Micra stamped into Charlie's brain in seconds.

Then we chugged and jerked down the avenue.

I don't know what prompted me to look back – maybe it was the thought that I should be back there on the date of a lifetime, maybe even in Jamie's arms – but I nearly died when I saw Simon standing on the steps watching us. And I died again – on the double – when I saw him hurry towards Cass's car.

'Simon's seen us,' I announced. 'I think he's coming after us.'

'That's all we need,' said Jamie, straining to look back. 'But it figures.'

'What do you mean?' I asked, my voice jumping along with Charlie's jerky driving.

'With Dave off the list – he'd hardly sabotage the plane he's driving – that leaves Simon.'

That realisation caused a third heart tremor.

I'd had enough of that, thank you. 'Get a move on, Charlie,' I shouted. 'Can't you manage this thing?'

'I'm trying,' said Charlie. 'Nearly have the hang of it. Hold on.' And with that he swung out on to the main road to the town – on the wrong side.

'Charlie, we drive on the left!' I screamed.

'Sorry,' muttered Charlie, straightening the car as Jamie and I breathed a sigh of relief.

I glanced back. Simon was still at the gates, waiting for a break in traffic. By now Charlie really did have the hang of things and we were travelling smoothly.

'Watch the speed limit, Charlie,' advised Jamie as we approached the roundabout. 'Don't want the cops after us. We'd never be able to explain what we're doing.'

'Plus the fact that I'm supposed to be under some sort of "hotel arrest",' muttered Charlie. 'And that I have no driver's licence, we're not insured and this car has been taken without the owner's permission. Stolen, not to put too fine a point on it.'

'Oh cripes!' I sighed. I was in this right up to my elegant neck. Jamie clicked open the glove compartment in front of him and suddenly got very excited.

'A phone!' he exclaimed. 'Ragnell's left her mobile!'

'Oh, wow!' I said. 'Now we can ring the airport.'

But Jamie was shaking his head.

'What?' I asked. 'What's wrong?'

'It's a Panasonic Digifone,' he replied, holding the dash as Charlie swerved around the roundabout.

'So? What about it? It's a phone isn't it? What difference what make it is?'

'It needs a pin number,' went on Jamie. 'We can't use it.'

I leaned forward, as if my staring at the stupid thing was going to make a difference. As Jamie reached out to put it back in the glove compartment, something caught my eye. 'Is that an address book?' I asked, pointing over his shoulder. 'Yes,' he said. 'But what use…'

'Give it to me,' I went on. 'Quick, just do it.'

With doubt on his face, he handed it back to me. I quickly riffled through the pages. 'I knew it!' I exclaimed with as much glee as one can muster in these crazy circumstances. 'This has to be it. Try these numbers.' And, as I called them out to Jamie, he punched them in.

'Got it!' he cried in amazement. 'We have a tone! We're in. How did you do that, Maeve?' I smiled to myself. I'd figured that, if Ragnell was any way like me, she'd have her pin written in the address book, just like I do. Right under P for pin. You know about me and numbers – if they're not written down they dissolve in my brain. See? Maybe I still had a lot to learn about being as cool as Ragnell, but underneath we were two of a kind.

'Which way now?' roared Charlie.

'Dublin,' Jamie and I said together. 'We'll be on the motorway after the next roundabout,' I added. 'So just keep to the signs for Dublin.'

While Jamie punched in more numbers, I glanced behind. No sign of Simon. The breath of relief that was on its way to my lungs was rudely halted when the car behind passed us on a curve and I could see the dusty Opel Astra several cars back.

I said nothing. No point in creating panic. Not yet. Not while Jamie was talking on the phone. He'd got through to Directory Enquiries and was asking the number for Dublin airport. Of course Charlie and I could only hear Jamie's side of the conversation. And it wasn't going very well, by the sound of it. The fragmented conversation was, 'Cessna' ... 'sabotaged' ... 'sugar' ... 'should have arrived over an hour ago'... 'any report of a plane going down?'

My heart lurched at that one. Could Dave have done as Charlie suggested and changed from the good tank to the sabotaged one? Leo's laughing face suddenly became very dear to me. I wished he was right here right now annoying the life out of us and I wouldn't mind at all. Would I see him again, or was he spread across some field? I smothered a sob and looked back. I almost wanted Charlie to stop so that I could tear that crook, Simon, limb from limb. But that wasn't very constructive thinking.

Jamie pressed the shut-down key and shook his head in exasperation as he thrust the phone into his pocket.

'Got through to security,' he muttered angrily. 'They thought it was a hoax. Then they said that there was no Cessna anywhere in the airport.'

'Oh no.' Here was my worst fear being voiced, which made it more credible coming from Jamie. 'Could it already have gone down?' My voice was verging on the hysterical. 'Could it be that they never made it...?'

Jamie turned back to look at me. 'Don't even think

like that,' he said. 'Focus, Maeve. Focus on what we *can* do.'

Charlie, meanwhile, was edging into the fast lane on the motorway. Behind us, Simon was doing likewise.

'He's gaining on us,' I said. 'Simon. He's catching up.'

Charlie's mouth pressed to grim determination. 'My foot's down as far as it'll go,' he said. 'I don't think this car is in the whole of its health.'

'What's he after anyway?' said Jamie. 'How does he expect to stop us?'

'He's American, remember,' I said bitterly. 'Probably has a gun tucked into his boxers. They're all gun-mad, those Yanks. They think the gun is the answer to everything.'

Oops! Wry look from American Charlie in the mirror. Wrong thing to say, Maeve. But Charlie just nodded and went back to concentrating on his driving.

'Don't be such a drama queen, Maeve,' said Jamie. 'We've enough problems.'

'Yeah, well don't forget that this is the psychopath who emptied a bag of sugar into the engine of a plane. You're … you're sure about that, aren't you Charlie?'

Charlie was leaning forward, gripping the steering wheel as he passed a big artic. 'I used to be a crop-duster during college holidays.'

'A what?'

'A crop-duster,' explained Jamie. 'Small planes that fly over crops and spray pesticide on them. Go on, Charlie.'

'Well, it wasn't unknown in some places for rival crop-dusters to sabotage each other's planes. Sugar was the usual method. You learn to look out for the signs. We'd look for sugar grains before loading up. Believe me, I know how to spot sabotage and that plane was sabotaged.'

'But why?' I wondered aloud. 'Why would he want to kill three innocent people?'

'Who knows?' shrugged Jamie. 'Let's just concentrate on getting to that airport.'

My neck was getting stiff from the anxious twisting I was doing to keep Simon in sight. I could just make him out at the tail end of the traffic behind us. And wishing with all my heart that he wasn't in sight. Please let him crash, I thought. Not enough to kill him, just enough to break a leg or two so that he can be charged with attempted murder. I kept the emphasis on the word *attempted*. The alternative was too awful to contemplate.

We were off the motorway, on a stretch of country road way beyond Portlaoise when the car began to chug. 'Oh good lord!' exclaimed Jamie.

'What?' said Charlie, eyes still on the road.

'Petrol,' replied Jamie, desperately tapping the fuel gauge. 'We're out of petrol! Never thought to check.'

'And in the middle of nowhere,' added Charlie with frustration in his voice as the car chugged again.

'It's no use,' said Jamie. 'You're going to have to pull in to the grass margin. We couldn't risk getting stuck on a stretch with no margin. One of us will have to hitch a lift to the nearest garage.'

There was a bump as Charlie drove as far into the ditch as was possible. We all leapt out. Jamie tried flagging down the cars immediately behind, but the mean prats ignored him. Then Simon came into view. There was a screech of brakes as he pulled up. Now what? I braced myself for whatever madness was going to come our way. Jamie reached out and grabbed my hand.

'Get ready to run,' he said.

17

Emergency Dash

Simon jumped from his car and beckoned frantically to us. 'Come on!' he shouted. 'Get in, quickly.'

'What?' Charlie shouted back. I could see his hands clenched into fists, ready for action.

'For heaven's sake!' Simon shouted again. 'Get in. There's no time to lose.'

'What'll we do, Charlie?' asked Jamie.

'Stay there,' said Charlie. 'I'll see what he wants.'

Other cars were whizzing past. I wondered what their owners would do if they knew the awful fix we were in. I swore never to let my father or mother pass troubled people on the road again. If I lived to see my father and mother, that is. I made a feeble attempt to flag down a couple of cars while Charlie made his way to Simon.

'What do we do if ... if a fight breaks out between those two?' I asked Jamie.

'We run like hell,' replied Jamie. 'We're dealing with a madman. If Charlie can't deal with him, our only hope is to get help.'

'Hey!' I cried. 'Look, Charlie's waving us on.'

Jamie hesitated. I could see that suspicious expression on his face. He was wondering if this could be a set-up. Well, we'd been through so much madness already that it was easy to see how one would wonder who to trust.

'It's all right,' Charlie called out. 'Lock the car and come on. Hurry.'

'Better do as he says,' I said, tugging Jamie's sweater. 'It can't get much worse, can it?'

We reluctantly made our way to Simon's car. Charlie pulled open the rear door. 'Get in,' he said. 'Now.' he added, giving me a bit of a push as I hesitated.

No going back now. Jamie hadn't even pulled the door shut when Simon revved up and we were off again. We waited for someone to speak, Jamie and me, afraid to ask questions in case we mightn't like the answers.

'It's Cass,' said Simon, when we were back on course.

'What about Cass?' I asked suspiciously.

'She's the cause of all this,' said Charlie. 'Go on, Simon, tell us.'

'Cass is...' Simon hesitated. 'Cass has problems.' He stopped again. Oh great, we were on our way to find out if three people were dispersed across some field, and Cass had a problem. What a worry. Was it bad breath? Ingrowing ear hair? Boils on her bum? I snorted and was about to say something really profound when Simon cleared his throat and spoke again. 'Cass spent many years in secure care back in the States,' he went on.

'What do you mean "secure care"?' I asked.

'I think he means a psychiatric hospital, one for people who've comitted crimes,' said Charlie. 'Would I be right?' Simon nodded.

'She was a top accountant,' went on Simon. 'Working for a light airplane company.'

'Airplane company!' I spluttered, looking meaningfuly at Jamie, but he was focused on Simon.

'At the height of her career, when she got greedy,' went on Simon. 'She embezzled some money – actually a lot of money.'

'Ha, just like old JA,' I couldn't resist saying. Jamie nudged me to be silent.

'When it was discovered,' continued Simon, 'she attacked the director who tried to hush the affair by confronting her privately in his office. She attacked him in a frenzy, left him for dead. It turned out that the same thing had happened in a previous job back when she was in her twenties. Only, in that case somebody died. She got away with it that time, the verdict was an accident.'

'But this time?' I asked.

Simon shook his head. I wished he wouldn't do that. Driving and head-shaking are better done on separate occasions. 'When it happened again,' he went on, 'the past caught up with her. She was diagnosed as a severe schizophrenic. It was as if money and violence went together to create a sort of madness. And that's how she came to us.'

'To us? What do you mean "to us"?' I asked as Simon slowed down coming in to Monastrevin.

'To the hospital where I worked as a nurse. That's how I met Cass.'

And so, in that long drive we learnt the the story of Cass Carstairs. She was the only sister of Dave's dad. Both Dave's parents had been killed in a car accident ten years ago, leaving him as heir to Goodnight House.

Goodnight House was always foremost in Cass's thoughts all that time she was incarcerated in the hospital. She'd built up a special bond with Simon and told him all about her childhood there and how she longed to go back. In one of her confessional moods, she'd told him the family secret about how JA Carstairs had come by his money, and even about the theft of the fan. The next day she had denied it, of course. All those years, she was responding to treatment and it was eventually decided that she was cured and could go back into society. When she asked Simon if he'd come to Ireland with her, to her beloved Goodnight House, he agreed. He was in his late fifties and was thinking of retiring anyway. That was four years ago.

Everything was going fine until two things happened together. The first was when she met Charlie at Ragnell's opening. She recognised the family resemblance from the photo – she had had that photo always at her bedside back in America – and all the old fears of the source of the Carstairs fortune being revealed caused her to sink into the paranoia that goes with schizophrenia. The crunch came when Dave declared his engagement.

'That's why you dropped the jug that night,' I put in. 'You knew it would send her back to the screaming habdabs.'

Simon nodded. We were fairly belting along. By now we were at the Red Cow roundabout, turning left for the airport.

Anyway, to get back to the Cass saga: all she could see ahead was losing her place in Goodnight House forever when Dave and Ragnell married and had a family. She couldn't bear the thoughts of that. Simon had tried to console her, to tell her that Dave wouldn't put her out, that there was room in the big house for everyone. But Cass was sinking and Simon began to realise that she was getting out of control. The two things, Charlie's appearance and Dave's engagement, drove her to extremes. It was she who took the key from Dave's pocket that night. She had known he always had it with him.

'But why steal the fan?' asked Jamie. 'And the money as well?'

'Because she didn't want Charlie to see it and make the connection between it and Goodnight House,' replied Simon. 'The money was just to make it look like a genuine theft.'

'Huh, she didn't know that Charlie had already seen

the fan,' I said.

'And that I knew already about Goodnight House,' added Charlie. 'Her reasoning was pathetic.'

Simon nodded. 'Just remember she was in a state of diminished responsibility,' he said. 'Nothing she did made sense.'

'You mean she was a bit of a mad hatter?' I said. I like things to be straightforward.

'Something like that,' replied Simon.

'So it was she who hid that photo with Charlie's ancestor on it?' I said. 'I thought that was you. And I suppose that night, when Dave rang for you to put in the plane, you were out looking for Cass?'

'Do you mean the night of the break-in?' asked Simon. 'I didn't know Dave had rung, but yes, I was out looking for Cass. I knew she had broken in to take the fan, but what could I do? Who could I tell without creating chaos?'

'You should have,' I said. 'Chaos or not, we wouldn't be sitting here now afraid to think of what might have happened. Did you not know she'd put sugar in the plane so that ... so that she'd have her stupid monstrosity of a house all to herself...'

I broke off, couldn't say any more.

'I only found out just now,' said Simon. 'She saw you three from the window and said you'd never make it. I asked her what she meant and she laughed and started to rant about 'sugary engines' and how we'd soon have the place to ourselves. I knew then what she had done and rang Dublin airport. They said there were no Cessnas in the airport, and started referring me from one person to another. I couldn't wait, knew I'd have to do this myself. And here we are. Let's just hope we get there in time.'

'We need coins,' said Jamie. 'Toll ahead.'

We scrabbled for loose change and waited impatiently in the queue, each of us absorbing the horrendous story of Cass and her love for an old barn of a house that had driven her to possible murder. I swallowed hard and felt like getting out and shouting to all the drivers of all the cars around us that they must help us.

We finally got to the airport. Simon drove straight to a security booth. The conversation was brief. Privately owned small aircraft were discouraged from landing, in Dublin airport except in very special circumstances. 'Far too busy to allow small craft,' went on the security man. 'They'd be a danger to the commercial flights.'

'Where is there a landing-strip for private planes?' Charlie leaned across, desperation in his voice.

The security man scratched his head. 'Depends on where the plane is coming from,' he said.

'The west midands,' shouted Jamie.

'Probably Leixlip,' said the security man. 'Weston landing strip in Leixlip. That's where most of west and midlands small aircraft land.'

We didn't wait to explain. Simon did a U-turn and belted back the way we'd come. 'Where the hell is Leixlip?' he asked.

Well, there was only me to know, since I was the only native. 'County Kildare,' I said. 'Head back towards Kildare, there should be a signpost for Maynooth and Leixlip.' I hoped I was right. I'd been along that route several times, but as far as I was concerned roads are just lines from A to B. A thought struck me. 'How come you didn't know which airport Dave was heading for, Simon?' I asked.

Simon shook his head slightly. 'Because I'm terrified of flying,' he said. 'I don't have anything to do with the plane. Besides, Dave and I get along just fine, but we keep a comfortable distance from each other – he has his interests and I have mine.'

'Does he know about … about Cass and all that trouble?' I went on.

Simon didn't reply as he negotiated passing out two cars. 'No,' he then said. 'He just accepted Cass's story about her business going bust. I didn't see the need to enlighten him. As far as I was concerned, Cass was cured and deserved a chance of a new life.'

Jamie glanced at his watch and gave me an apprehensive look. 'What time is?' I asked. I didn't really want to know, but it's one of those questions you'd ask automatically anyway.

'Getting on for half past four,' he said.

'Oh lord,' I groaned. 'They'll be leaving soon. We'll never make it.'

'Don't say that,' grunted Simon. 'We'll make sure to get there.'

'The phone,' said Charlie. 'Did you leave the phone in the car?'

'No. I have it here,' replied Jamie, pulling it out of his pocket. 'I'll get the number for that airfield. What's it called again?'

'Weston,' Charlie and I said together.

We travelled in tense silence while Jamie got on to Directory Enquiries. Everything will be all right now, I told myself, trying to keep the image of Leo's moony face foremost in my mind. His live and moony face. I looked anxiously at Jamie. What was keeping him? Why were no words being spoken across the airwaves. He gave an exasperated sigh.

'What's wrong?' I asked. 'Is there no answer?'

Jamie shook the phone helplessly. 'Bloody batteries are gone.'

If he had hit me with a sock filled with wet cement it wouldn't have been half as devastating as that statement. 'Oh, Jamie,' I said, putting my knuckles in my mouth.

'It's down to us getting there now,' said Simon grimly. 'Hold on.'

With that we speeded up, passing everything in sight. Normally the blur of passing landscape at that speed would have been enough to have me clawing the roof, but the tension and urgency gave my head a whole different set of priorities.

'Try again,' I said to Jamie.

'No point,' he said dismally. 'It needs recharging.'

Living in Dublin, as I do, I'm pretty used to the sound of a police siren. You learn to ignore it. But Charlie and Jamie both twisted around. A look of horror crossed Charlie's face. 'That's all we need.'

'What?' I said, turning also. Coming after us was a cop car, blue light flashing. 'Probably after someone,' I said. 'You often see…'

'They're after us,' muttered Simon. 'I'm way over the speed limit.'

The panic that I'd had on a leash since this whole horrible business started began to break free. Heart, stomach, lungs all started to kick in. Not to mention the steel bands tightening on my head from the inside. 'Let's stop and explain,' I said, knowing, even as I said it, that it was a stupid thing to say.

Simon's knuckles were white as he gripped the steering-wheel even tighter.

'By the time it took to convince them it might be too late,' said Charlie. 'We can't leave anything to chance.'

Now my breaths were coming in short gasps. It was like dry drowning.

Jamie leaned over and grabbed my two hands. 'Look

at me, Maeve,' he said. I swallowed another mouthful of air and did as he said. 'It will be all right,' he said evenly. 'We'll get there. Just keep that in mind. Even if they've started to take off, the airfield will get the message to them.'

Fat consolation that was, even if he was holding my hands. 'But if they press that selector button on the second fuel tank,' I said, trying to control my wobbly voice, 'then they'll crash.'

'Airfield's ahead,' called Charlie.

Sure enough, there it was: Weston airfield. Simon swerved into the avenue. Behind us, the garda car swerved as well. Ahead of us there was a gate. A *closed* gate.

'Damn!' swore Simon.

Before the car had even stopped, Charlie was out, pushing the gate. But it was too late. The garda car screeched to a halt, two gardai hopped out and were on us in a flash of fluorescent waistcoats. Everyone froze. Ahead of us, tantalisingly near, was the airfield.

'Out,' said a very annoyed garda. 'I want your driving licence, and a very good explanation for your dangerous driving. Out! Now!'

With an air of defeated resignation, we crawled out. Simon and Charlie began their unreal account. This would take until a week of Sundays to get across, I thought. And in the meantime my cousin Leo and his step-aunt and her new fiancé were going to be splattered ....

'Bloody sure they won't,' I said aloud. And with that I hopped over the gate and ran towards the airfield. I was just conscious of a shout behind me and, out of the corner of my eye, a flash of fluorescence. I was being chased. Running flat out, I knew I'd never make it

against someone whose training was to outrun slippery criminals, never mind a fourteen-year-old girl whose sole physical training was circumnavigating the shopping mall.

There was another cry. This time I looked and was amazed to see Jamie's flying tackle as he brought my pursuer down. Rugby is one fantastic game, I thought. Bless it. But I also knew that this would only buy me a few seconds extra time. I kept going, legs like over-charged pistons. Dashed through the office doors, only vaguely aware of someone else shouting at me. Out on to the tarmac.

'Oh no,' I groaned desperately. There were forty or fifty small aircraft scattered about. I just kept running wildly. Now there were other voices too and, over them, the sound of an engine. I turned to where that sound was coming from and saw a small plane heading for the runway. Cutting across the grass I ran towards it. Maybe it was Dave's plane, maybe it wasn't. They all looked the same to me. Please let it not be, I prayed. Let them still be stationary. But I had to make sure. It was turning now, ready to speed up and take off. Come on, legs, move. I was near enough now to see a face at a window. There was no mistaking that moony face.

'Leo!' I screamed. But I might as well have been shouting into a bundle of feather pillows. I waved, screamed, and kept on running, my legs now on automatic.

Suddenly the head turned. At first there was disbelief, then a grin. He waved back. The silly twit, I thought in panic. Did he think I'd travelled all this distance just to see him go up in a cruddy plane?

'Stop!' I screamed again, giving a cross-arm windmill wave like you'd see in movies when someone wants someone else to stop. By now I was sobbing. Me, Maeve, poet and all-round tough lady, about to be reduced to a blubbering failure as my cousin and a couple of lovers were splattered on the runway. I sank on to the grass, head in hands. By now there were multifarious footsteps bearing down. Fluorescent waistcoats, dungarees, Jamie's Timberland boots. Falling, smell of grass.

Thunk! Sweet darkness.

18

Epilogue

'It suits you,' I whispered. Jamie glared at me with his one good eye. The other one was closed and had a ring of bright red around it that would darken to a nice shade of blue. 'Makes you look sort of heroic.'

'Heroic?' he laughed. 'Bringing down a policeman who has a steely uppercut isn't heroic, it's madness.'

'Ah, but it was your madness that gave Maeve that extra bit of time,' said Dave. 'We'd have been in the air if...' he didn't finish. We'd had enough of those 'ifs' and 'whatabouts', thanks very much.

'I don't think we'll forget this engagement in a hurry,' said Ragnell, holding out her left hand. Yeah sure, the ring sparkled, as things with diamonds stuck in them tend to, but I could never understand the fuss that goes with a shiny thing on your finger. 'This has to be potentially the most expensive ring ever,' she went on. 'Three lives would have been a huge price to pay.'

It was three o'clock in the morning. We were sitting around the kitchen table in Ragnell's place. Instead of the banquet in Chez George, we'd been eating fish and chips from bags. Never had food tasted so good. There's nothing like discovering that you're still alive to heighten the most trivial pleasures. Except sugar. I never wanted to taste sugar ever again.

'But it didn't happen,' said Charlie quietly. 'And that's the thought to keep uppermost.'

There was a short ring on the doorbell. 'Simon,' said Dave. Suddenly we were all tense again. Jamie got up to let him in. Simon looked worn out as Jamie led him into the kitchen. We all looked at him expectantly.

'She's settled in,' he said. Nobody said anything. Well, what was there to say? Is it a nice hospital? Are there pretty murals of mountains and butterflies? 'They'll keep her there for a while and then she'll be moved to a bigger hospital,' he went on wearily. 'I'm afraid she's beyond my care now.'

Well, that sure threw a damp and dirty tea-towel over our jubilation at being alive. Dave reached out and pressed Simon's arm. 'You did all you could,' he said.

'Will she go to jail?' asked Leo.

Simon shook his head. 'No. She'll just spend a long time in care.'

Leo looked disappointed, no doubt feeling cheated out of being able to boast that his young step-aunt's fiancé's old aunt was doing time for trying to kill him.

Well, personally I just hoped they'd have strong locks wherever this special care place was. Ones that would last a very long time. At least as long as my lifetime. I didn't want freaky nightmares about Cass coming after the one who'd ruined her plans. Well OK, I was just one of the rescuers, but in the long run it was me who stopped that plane. And I'd make sure that Leo would never forget it.

THE BEAUTIFUL HEROINE

By Maeve Morris

'Stop!' she cried. 'Don't fly that plane!
It's sabotaged by a dame insane.'
She threw herself upon the ground,
As voices shouted all around.
The wheels came closer. Would she die?

But lo! Who comes with big black eye?
Her hero bravely pulled her free.
Then down he went upon one knee.
'My dear,' he said. 'I know it's late.
But how about that great hot date?'

Well, with Leo back on the scene, my date with Jamie vanished back into the recesses of my mind as something to be wished for. It was back to practising scintillating conversation in the mirror. Of course there were times I wished that maybe Leo would have had to take to the bed for a few precious days to recover from his near-death experience. But, on the contrary, it seemed to make him more annoyingly alive than ever. However, I'm a kind-hearted person and there was no harm at all in curses I heaped on his head.

Charlie went back to the States with his precious fan. We all went to see him off. Dave apologised for his thieving ancestor. He wished the story hadn't been kept from him all those years, but Charlie was really nice about it. He was just thrilled to have the fan back, and didn't ask for a chunk of money from the proposed sale of Goodnight House. Yes, that's what I said. Dave said he couldn't live in that heap of gaudy stones any more and decided to put it up for sale. It would eventually be bought by a hotel group with plans for a sort of country club. The sort of place for pop-star weddings and *Hello!* or *VIP* magazine pictures.

And, speaking of weddings, Ragnell asked me to be a bridesmaid at hers. I thought seriously about that for a nano second. 'Will I have to wear a pink meringue and flowers?' I asked.

Ragnell laughed. 'You can wear pink docs, tattoos and flares if you like.'

'Well, in that case I'll do it,' I said. 'Just for you.'

And Simon? Well, as I had so cleverly forecast, the craft shop was pushed farther and farther down Ragnell's list of important things – one of those 'it-seemed-like-a-good-idea-at-the-time' cases. The plan was that after she and Dave married they'd spend a few years going around the world. Simon, who for some daft reason loved Ireland in spite of its dodgy weather, was given the option of renting the shop. He was thrilled. He said he'd always wanted to run a bookshop, that he'd sell some crafts and a lot of books.

'They'll probably do a lot better than crafts,' said Ragnell.

'Just make sure to get fun stuff,' I added. 'This town is a dead end as far as entertainment goes.'

Simon smiled and promised to get in loads of teenage books. Not that I'm big into books, being a poet who writes my own words and all that, but one has to look out for one's peers.

We went up to have a last look at Goodnight House on the day before we left, Jamie, Leo and me.

'I'll bet old James Aloysius is revolving in his grave right now,' I said. 'When he's not having a red-hot pitchfork shoved at his bum by one of Satan's lads.' And that was a very satisfying thought to be sure.

'What are you going to tell your grandad when he comes to collect you tomorrow?' said Leo. 'How will you explain that black eye?'

Jamie laughed, his good eye twinkling. 'I'll tell the truth,' he said. 'I'll tell him how Maeve and I, along with a Native American Indian and a crazy woman's minder chased after a sabotaged plane and that I had to tackle down a policeman who was chasing Maeve after we'd been done for speeding. Just your ordinary, everyday happening.'

'And that you nearly did your back in as well,' added Leo.

'What do you mean?' I asked. 'Did I miss out on something?'

Leo laughed and nudged Jamie. 'That time you conked out,' he said. 'Jamie insisted on carrying you off the grass. Wouldn't let anyone else help. Oh, look. There's Dave. Hi, Dave!' He ran ahead of us to where Dave was standing on the steps.

Jamie was blushing a nice puce to blend in with the eye. He looked at me with embarrassment.

My own eyes turned to saucers. 'You did?' I said.

Jamie nodded. 'That was a brave thing you did,' he muttered. 'I was dead proud.'

Well, if there had been no orchestra that day on our way to the river, there were heavenly choirs ringing in my ears right now. I gave a contented sigh. 'Just like in *Gone With the Wind*,' I said, looking up at Goodnight House. 'When that Butler guy picked up Charlotte O'Hara in his arms.'

Jamie laughed. 'I think you mean Scarlett.'

'Whatever,' I replied.

What did it matter? Even if I'd known nothing about it, I'd been in Jamie's arms after all. Now, what could possibly rhyme with 'mad delight'? Fantasy knight? Nah. Who needed fantasy, I thought, as I looked at my real-life, one-eyed hero.

END

MARY ARRIGAN lives in Roscrea, County Tipperary. As well as writing books for teenagers, she has written and illustrated books in Irish for younger children.

Her awards include the Sunday Times/CWA Short Story Award 1991; the Hennessy Award 1993; International Youth Library choice for White Ravens 1997; Bisto Merit Award 2000.

This is her seventh book for the Children's Press. The others are *Dead Monks and Shady Deals* (1995), *Landscape with Cracked Sheep* (1996), *Seascape with Barber's Harp* (1997), *The Spirits of the Bog* (1998), *Maeve and the Long-Arm Folly* (1999), *The Spirits of the Attic* (2000)